THE SHE-KING: BOOK FOUR

THE BULL
OF MIN

LIBBIE HAWKER

Cover design: Running Rabbit Press
Cover art: Joelle Douglas

Running Rabbit Press
Seattle, WA

ALSO BY THIS AUTHOR

THE SHE-KING SERIES
The Sekhmet Bed: Book One
The Crook and Flail: Book Two
Sovereign of Stars: Book Three

TIDEWATER
A Novel of Pocahontas and the Jamestown Colony

BAPTISM FOR THE DEAD

DAUGHTER OF SAND AND STONE
A Novel of Empress Zenobia
(Forthcoming, November 2015)

CONTENTS

THE SHE-KING: BOOK FOUR

THE BULL
OF MIN

O my mother Nut, goddess of the night sky, stretch thyself over me. Place me among the imperishable stars which are in thee, that I may not die.

-Inscription from the sarcophagus of Hatshepsut, fifth king of the Eighteenth Dynasty

PROLOGUE

THE MORNING SUN CAME WEAKLY over the garden wall. The old, disused wing of Waset's sprawling palace was overshadowed by taller structures, high roofs and the soaring, angular arches of gateway pylons. Deep violet shade cast everything in gloom, even at Re's golden dawning. Neferure crouched in her garden doorway, back against the stone, knees drawn to her chest. The scuff of footsteps high on the wall above mingled with birdsong as the guard on the roof walked his rounds. The birdsong was thin and faint, distant. No birds came to Neferure's garden. It was bare and inhospitable, dry and desolate.

Thutmose had kept her here in solitude for nearly two months. Neferure counted the days, first wondering with a quiet calm when her imprisonment would come to an end, as it must surely, someday. It made no sense for her brother to keep her secluded indefinitely. What purpose could she serve here? Even the spirit of vengeance that prompted her husband to isolate her in a forgotten corner of the palace could not be satisfied forever by imprisonment.

The weeks dragged on, though, and Neferure remained confined. Soon she found herself pacing and panting like a leopard in a menagerie cage. A servant brought her meals and oil for her skin, carried away her chamber pot covered in a tidy cloth. But how long until the servant forgot – until Thutmose forgot, engrossed as he was with a Pharaoh's duties? Even the soldiers prowling the walls would forget to walk their endless, silent circuits, and Neferure's abandonment would be complete. She would starve or perish of thirst, clawing desperately at the perfectly smooth, unclimbable walls of her prison.

But no. That would not be her fate. It was not a fitting end for Hathor's handmaid, for the consort of a god, to rot in forgotten captivity. Today she would go free, or die trying.

The hinge of her chamber door creaked. The servant woman appeared, timid and suspicious as always, hunched over her tray. Beyond the woman's furtive frame, the door guard stood alert and immovable.

"Good day to you," Neferure said sweetly.

She remained huddled on the garden threshold as the woman, unspeaking, set about her duties. The servant left the tray in its usual spot, on the hard, narrow bed against one wall, and deposited a new jar of bath oil on the floor.

"You may go," Neferure whispered, though there was no need to dismiss the woman. She went every day when her work was finished, whether Neferure willed it or no.

When the door swung closed, Neferure eased herself to her feet. Her muscles and bones ached from remaining crouched so long – from remaining captive so long. She gazed with some regret at the little Hathor shrine standing opposite the bed, its offering bowl cold and empty, ringed with a bit of pale ash from last night's prayers. *I must leave you, Lady*, she said in her heart, sorrowing. For the goddess herself lived in the seven small statues arrayed on her shrine – or a tiny bit of her lived there. From the seven statues, the Lady of the West had watched Neferure's confusion and solitude, had been her only companion in the darkness. It was a bitter thing, to leave Hathor behind. But Neferure would be able to carry nothing with her.

It is time to go.

She ate methodically, tasting nothing of the sweet cakes and fruit, thinking only to fuel her body for the task ahead.

In the small, unadorned bath, Neferure stepped down

into the sunken tub. The closed sluice stood at chest height in the sandstone wall, a few beads of water leaking from its corners. Neferure breathed deeply to steady herself, then seized the handle of the sluice door in shaking hands. She pulled upward with all her strength. The cedar planks of the little door had swelled with the moisture of the ducts, and with the pressure of the bathwater it held back. It resisted her. She crouched, braced her hands and one shoulder against the handle, strained against the door, the muscles in her legs and back crying out. The sluice gave way all at once, and she gasped as she stumbled backward, the cascade of water forceful against her thighs, plastering her dress to her legs.

Neferure watched the water pour from the duct. The flow was strong, but as the water collecting in the tub edged up above her ankles, she was certain she saw now what she had only thought she'd noted on previous days. The rush of water was slowing. Not by much – not yet. But the flow decreased enough to give her hope.

She scrambled from the tub and kicked off her sandals, shed her dress and wig, shoved them far beneath the stone bench against the bath's wall. Then she stood shivering with excitement and fear as the water level rose in the sunken tub, and slowed yet more from the mouth of the sluice. The water in this duct in this old wing of the palace must have long since been diverted for some other, more important source. A continual supply would not be spared for a disused room such as this one. Thutmose must have overlooked it – must have neglected to order the ducts fully opened when he moved Neferure in. The water she bathed in each day must be some sort of overflow, a finite daily supply, if the slackening volume from the sluice was anything to judge by. The only question that taunted her was whether it would slow enough to allow her to escape before it flooded the room, seeping beneath the door into the hallway outside, alerting the door guard and bringing Thutmose and Hatshepsut down upon Neferure before she could break free.

The tub was three quarters full now. The flow of water had reduced until it ran down the wall rather than spurting outward with force. *I must go now – now!* Neferure seized the jar of bath oil and upended it over her shoulders, smeared it quickly across her back and shoulders until her skin and hands were slick. Then she splashed across the tub, the water lapping mid-thigh, and braced her hands in the mouth of the sluice.

The duct looked barely wide enough for her to wriggle inside. There was a shallow lip in the stone; she hauled her head and shoulders up into the dark passage, cringing from the fearful roar of moving water echoing against black stone. Her slick fingers slipped, and she thrashed her legs, caught a hold on the edge of the tub with one toe, and slowly, painfully squeezed her thin body deep into the duct.

Inside, pressed flat by the constricting walls, unable to see, she arched her neck painfully backward to keep her nose clear of the water. The crown of her head scraped against stone. She kicked her legs feebly, and her heel caught on the sluice door. With a rasping grate, it dropped back into place.

There is no going back now. I find my way out, or I die.

With arms stretched before her and face barely clear of the water, Neferure inched against the water's flow, pushing with bruised toes, pulling with frantic, clawing fingers. She prayed to Hathor that the duct was as good as dry, that the closed sluice would not cause this tunnel to refill and drown her. It was a very narrow and unfriendly tomb. She writhed like an eel, pushing herself forward desperately, forward, forward as the water rose to cover her mouth. Her breath rasped through her nostrils. But the oil on her skin and the slime coating the walls of the duct freed her movement. She raced against the refilling water while her heart roared in her ears.

In the blackness she detected a louder roaring: an adjoining duct. Neferure's hands fell off the lip of her duct into cold, wet nothingness; she plunged momentarily below water, and struggled back, straining to keep her nose free, to breathe the chill, desperate air. She felt carefully with weak, shaking fingers. Her duct had come to an end, sure enough, emptying into a deeper passage. Craning her neck like a stork, she could just feel, with the scraped and bruised top of her head, where the duct's ceiling opened out into a larger pocket of air. She had found her way to a main tunnel, like the trunk of a tree from which many dark, cold branches sprouted. She eased herself forward into the deeper blackness, clinging to the lip of her narrow duct with desperate hands. As terrible and menacing as the passage was, in this impenetrable blackness it was the only thing familiar to her. Her toes just touched a soft silted floor. By taking bouncing steps, she could edge her face free of the waterline and suck in a desperate breath before falling back beneath the surface.

Neferure counseled herself to calmness, though her heart gibbered with panic. She held a lungful of air and sank beneath the water, one hand on the slimy wall. She felt the gentle flow of a slight current, heard a distant, muffled rushing somewhere to her left. With one last, desperate prayer to gods of water and air, she kicked away from the wall and swam into the unknowable blackness.

After a great eternity of gliding blind through the darkness, the breath burning in her lungs, Neferure's hands struck cold stone. She clawed against it, pulling herself in a direction she hoped was up, straining for the surface. *Please, Hathor, let me not have passed beneath a wall, let there be air above me – air!*

Hathor was good. Neferure burst from the surface with a desperate gasp. The air that filled her lungs was sweeter than honey on her tongue. She pawed at the wall, felt the stone give way to the smoother, slime-covered planks of a great cedarwood sluicegate. She could feel the gate vibrating faintly, moving with the strength of a healthy current on its other side. *It is my only possible way out. I must try it.* Groping, she found a gap at the top of the gate just above the waterline and hoped it was wide enough to admit her.

Her cheek and scalp scraped against the stone of the great duct's ceiling. The sluicegate forced the precious air from her lungs as she struggled through the gap. Below her she could feel the deeper chill of fast-moving water, hear it slapping and gurgling against the walls of the duct. And, with a desperate wonder, she realized that she could *see* the surface of the water, a grey glimmer dancing before her disbelieving eyes. She caught one brief glimpse of daylight, a distant point sparkling golden in the echoing blackness of the tunnel, before she fell over the sluicegate and plunged again beneath the water. When she broke the surface again, gasping with weakness and triumph, swimming with feeble strokes against the flow of the current, she wept in gratitude and relief.

It was an easy enough thing to dive beneath the bronze grate at the duct's head, once she had clung to its bars for a long while, catching her breath, stilling the terrible quivering in her bones. Compared to swimming through the unknown dark or holding her head free of the rising water in her narrow tomb, it was the simplest thing she had ever done to press her body deep into the soft silt and writhe beneath the bars, kick against them with her small feet, pull herself hand over hand up into the air, the *light*, the blessed light.

Neferure dragged her exhausted body up the bank of the canal, heedless of the mud that coated her skin and stung in the cuts and scrapes along her back, her belly, her thighs. She curled into a sun-warmed hollow beneath an olive tree and slept, naked and vulnerable, until the wind in the branches woke her. When she made to rise, her muscles were so cramped and resistant that she cried out with a hundred pains. She was obliged to uncurl herself with great care, massaging her limbs, stretching them tentatively. The wind rattled the olive branches again. A bird called harshly above her, and she smiled to hear it. Both of them were free now, she and the bird. Nearby, the palace's outer walls had begun to glow red with the approaching sunset.

I must get away from here. They have realized by now that I am not in my chamber. They will be looking for me.

A line of trees and tall grasses ran along the bank of the canal, out from the palace's flank through spans of crop fields. She picked her way between the trunks of the trees, moving casually, not furtively, careful to look as nonchalant as any woman might who was naked and covered in a crust of dark dried mud. *The mud will help disguise me among the foliage*, she thought, hoping it was true. *I will be difficult to spot from the palace walls.*

The further she drew from the palace, the lighter her heart grew. Its sounds receded, the faint lift and echo of soldiers' voices calling the change of the guard, the more distant, murmuring music of the city of Waset, the voices in its marketplaces, the pounding of artisans' tools, the harsh, shrill singing of city women. A gentler song caressed her. Birds hopped and warbled in profusion among the trees, delighting her eyes with flashes of color, their feathers glimmering in the deep warmth of a lowering sun. An early chorus of frogs emerged from the reeds. Their voices joined in a haphazard, uncoordinated chant. The humble homes of rekhet farmers came into view, raised slightly above the fields on their little earthen hillocks. A mother called for her child from one of these homes, the voice mingling with birdsong. "Satiah! Satiah!"

The sun disappeared below the western horizon in a blaze of crimson. Purple night gathered over the fields. Neferure shivered, rubbed her hands briskly over her arms, crumbling her coating of mud to dust. Her stomach gnawed at her fiercely. She had eaten practically nothing all day, and had suffered a great trial by anyone's reckoning. The olives in the trees were still unripe, much too hard and bitter to eat. She paused, gazing out across the fields, uncertain and alone.

What shall I do, Hathor? I am yours. Direct me, and I shall go where you will, do as you will.

Neferure's feet turned toward the field to her right. She

hesitated among the tall grasses of the verge, plucking at the spiny seed heads with trembling hands. The palace, far behind her now, had darkened to a great gloomy shadow. The golden pinpoints of lamps flickered faintly along its wall. There was no way to know who might be hunting for her, or where. Yet she could not remain hidden in the grass forever. She would starve, and when the day came again, the high sun would burn her unprotected skin. There was nothing for it but to trust in the goddess, to go where she directed.

Neferure crossed the field. A mound of earth rose at the far end, and at its peak stood a small, humble rekhet hut. A friendly light glowed in its narrow, slitted windows. She kept her eyes fixed on that glow and moved calmly, her pace deliberate and serene, even when she heard the distant barking of hounds echo from the palace walls. The low sprouts of new grain brushed her ankles, tickled against her skin. She rubbed her body, doing her best to clear away the dried plaster of mud that had not shaken free as she had walked beneath the trees. Her fingers broke open a cut on her thigh, and it bled freely down her leg. Neferure kept moving.

When she gained the base of the hut's little hillock and gazed up at the home, its edges lost in the violet darkness, she paused in uncertainty. Should she clap at the door? Shout for help? And what would she tell the rekhet who lived within? She let her heart fall open to the gods, questioning, but there was no answer. As she waited servilely for inspiration, a shadow passed across the glow of one window. The silhouette halted its movement with a jerk, and a heartbeat later a woman's startled shriek split the night.

"Holy Iset!"

The hut's door flung open. A shaft of deep yellow light fell down the hill to land at Neferure's bruised and swollen feet.

"In, in! Come in, you poor creature!"

The deeper tones of a man's voice muttered something from within the hut, and the woman answered.

"It's a child – a girl. Look at her. You can see she's in a bad way. Come in, child, come in."

A hound bayed, the cry distorted by distance. It sounded as if it called from south side of the palace, far from this quiet hut. Neferure moved up the hill with growing confidence.

The woman, draped in a simple tunic of rough linen, enfolded Neferure in warm, plump arms. She was approaching middle age, if the lines of her face were any indication. Her eyelids closed and fluttered with the force of sympathy.

"Ah, gods, look at you! What a tattered thing you are, and thin as a minnow."

"By Sobek," the man's voice said from a dim corner, "we don't need another mouth to feed. Send the stray pup back to its dam."

The woman tutted. "Keep your cruel mouth shut, Baki." She scolded the man, but her voice was affectionate. "You can see the poor thing has been abused."

Neferure sighed and covered her face with her hands. She felt a gentle touch on her thigh, and the woman raised her fingers to examine the trace of blood she found there.

"Ah!" Her face twisted in disgust. "So that's the story. Some vile young men in rut found you in the fields, did they? No, don't speak. Don't say a word. It's the plight of women, my little thing, my poor minnow. You'll be all right with time."

"I say, send her away," Baki barked.

Now there was real anger in the woman's voice as she turned away to shout into the depths of her home. "Another word out of you, and I'll beat you with your own walking stick. The child stays. It is not a matter for discussion."

Baki made a disgusted noise deep in his throat.

The woman shut the door firmly on the night and the hounds, on the palace with its soldiers, with its thrones and Pharaohs. She tucked Neferure beneath a plump arm and guided her into the hut. A wool blanket was strewn across a rickety little couch woven of tough, dry reeds. She snatched it up and bundled it around Neferure, covering her nakedness.

"There. That's better. Baki, bring me a bit of that stew and some bread. And a jar of wine."

A rough man tending toward old age rose stiffly from a stool beside a rustic brazier. He shuffled off to an adjoining room, muttering beneath his breath about the costliness of wine.

"I am Harit," the woman said, easing Neferure down onto the woven couch. When Harit sat beside her, the couch's coarse reeds squeaked beneath the weight. "What is your name, child?"

Neferure hesitated. She had not thought so far ahead, had not considered that she must meet people sooner or later, must give them some plausible identity that would leave no trail back to the palace. Gaping, she cast about for a name, and the only one she had heard recently came at last to her lips.

"Satiah. I am Satiah."

The food arrived: an unremarkable stew of fish and onions, a piece of bread, and a clay cup of cheap, sour wine. Neferure gulped it all down gratefully, then finished off the hunk of coarse bread, picking crumbs from her blanket. Harit beamed her approval, then bedded Neferure down on the couch of creaking reeds.

Sleep was dreamless, deep, and healing. She woke renewed, blinking her eyes in a wan morning light that fought its way in through the narrow slit of the hut's window. Harit was already bustling about her morning chores, humming the simple repetitive phrases of a rekhet tune that Neferure did not know.

"You're awake. Good."

The woman brought her more bread topped with a meager chunk of honey still in the comb. Neferure ate it gratefully, chewing the earthy wax of the honeycomb until all the sweetness was gone. She donned the tunic and sandals Harit had laid out for her. Both were too large and the weave of the unbleached linen was inelegant and scratchy, but their plainness added to Neferure's disguise. She had no wig, but her natural hair had grown in somewhat during her confinement, and she did not look wholly out of place. Harit had also thoughtfully provided a simple head-cloth, the kind the rekhet wore in outdoor labor to ward off the worst of the sun's rays. Of course Neferure had never worn the like before, but she managed to fasten it with a tied linen band as confidently as if she had worn a head-cloth every day of her life.

She followed Harit out into the bare yard. The sun was still low and pale on the horizon. It cast long, cool shadows out into the field, where Neferure could make out the form of Baki stooping among the ankle-high sprouts, working at the earth with a long wooden pole. Harit handed her a crude bucket of leather stretched around a wooden hoop. A braid of dirty linen served as a handle.

"Water for the goats first," Harit said. "Then we make bread."

Neferure slung the bucket on her shoulder and stepped toward the footpath Harit indicated. It wended northward through the fields, paralleling the road on its raised causeway. Some hundred paces down the path, the canal's banks were less steep and the water flowed through a dark culvert beneath the road. Beyond, sitting like a throne upon the royal dais, the distant, pale walls of a large house and several outbuildings caught the rising sunlight, gleaming above a vast expanse of grape vines and the spread green blankets of new growth.

"What is that place?" Neferure asked, pointing.

Harit looked up from sweeping the threshold of her hut. "Don't you know? It's the estate of the Senenmut, the Great Royal Steward. Go on, now, little minnow. The goats cannot water themselves."

As she stared toward the great estate, her heart fell open like the petals of a flower beneath a hot, fierce sun. *There is a wrong to be righted*, a voice whispered inside her. She gasped at the sudden presence, trembling with joy. *Give me a sacrifice to soothe my anger. Spill the blood that is not divine, and the taint will pour out of your own blood. Then you will be purified, and worthy of me forever.*

Yes, Neferure replied. *I will do it. It will be as you say.*

She set her feet firmly upon the path

PART ONE

FALL
OF THE GOD

1464 B.C.E.

CHAPTER ONE

MERYET-HATSHEPSUT KEPT THE HEAVY CURTAINS of her litter tightly drawn. She climbed from the quay through the streets of Waset, the litter wending its way through streets choked with hawkers and craftsmen, children at play and women balancing baskets on their heads, messengers squeezing through the press with their masters' scrolls tucked beneath their arms. Hatshepsut rode ahead in a larger litter, a more ornate conveyance suitable for a Pharaoh, together with her women Batiret and Stire-In. As the litter tilted to gain the final hill before the palace gates, Meryet sank gratefully back onto her cushions, sighing, giving vent to the nameless emotion that tightened her chest. It was half sorrow, half relief. Sorrow for the sake of Hatshepsut. Relief on Meryet's own behalf, that she could draw her curtains and shut out, even for a short time, the terrible force of the Pharaoh's pain. Set apart from her king's grief as she now was, the distance felt as bracing as a cold drink of water in the heat of Shemu. And yet, having witnessed Hatshepsut's private sorrow, Meryet knew she could never be entirely free from the weight of it.

Grieving or not, Hatshepsut was a king to her very center. She did not betray her pain with a single tear, nor even the quiver of her lip – not where her subjects might see. The Pharaoh had wept and wailed her loss inside the echoing walls of Djeser-Djeseru while Meryet and the other women looked on, helpless in the face of a torment too great to ever be soothed. And yet when they boarded the ship to return to Waset's shore, Hatshepsut had been as still as a clouded pool, her face as impenetrable. Dutifully, Meryet had seated herself like a stone seshep beside Hatshepsut in the cabin of the boat, eyes forward, ignoring the sailors and guardsmen, the seabirds and the gaily leaping fish, as isolated and emotionless as the Pharaoh herself. It was the most difficult task Meryet had ever worked at, to keep her face expressionless. How could a woman remain so regal and calm when her heart split like an over-ripe fig, weeping all its sweetness away? *Will I ever learn to do it as easily as she does?* Meryet had wondered, cutting one sideways glance at Hatshepsut's unfeeling profile, stern as stone in the shade of the ship's canopy.

The litter moved from the mid-day sun to the deep, cool shadow beneath the pylons of the palace gate. Men's voices called and responded, the guards giving the correct signs to proceed into the Pharaoh's private realm. Lost and exhausted by her musings, Meryet did not hear the words, but only felt the brush of the cries against her senses, a faint tickle like a moth's wings in a twilight garden. When the litter sank to the ground in the courtyard she parted the curtains a finger's width.

As the bearers of the larger litter straightened, stretching their backs and arms, the fan-bearer Batiret emerged. Her pretty features were closed, forbidding, and none of the palace servants or ambassadors watching the arrival dared approach to make their bows to the king. Batiret offered her hand to her mistress, drew Hatshepsut from the veiled depths of her litter into the bright sun of the courtyard.

The Pharaoh was a woman in her middle years, thirty-six or −seven by Meryet's reckoning. Her form was more blocky than curved, powerful-looking even now, with shoulders stooped from exhaustion. The great sharp hook of her nose curved above a stern mouth edged with the lines of approaching age, and between her plucked and painted brows, two vertical tracks of worry had incised themselves permanently into her skin. Hatshepsut had never been pretty, not even as a girl – Meryet had seen that plainly from the moment she had first met the Pharaoh. But a woman's power did not reside in beauty, whatever the poets and singers might say. Hatshepsut's power was in her subtlety, her intelligence, which even now shone from her black eyes when her grief, so tightly and impossibly reined, did not. She could put her sorrow away before the eyes of her subjects and servants, but she could not put away the power she wore. It was as much a part of her as the confidence of her stride, the square and resolute posture of her shoulders, or the honey-brown color of her skin.

Hatshepsut raised a hand in a commanding gesture, and the guardsman Nehesi responded, moving swiftly to her side. The Pharaoh lifted the hem of her simple tunic dress and swept from the courtyard with her women in tow, her face an uncracked mask of power.

Meryet exhaled. She had not known she'd held her breath until Hatshepsut was gone. She left her own litter hastily, never seeing the bows of the servants and scribes through which she moved. Her body maids and personal guards fell in around her, silent and dutiful.

Meryet hesitated at the corridor that led to the chamber of the Great Royal Wife. The peaceful sanctuary of her own apartments beckoned to her. A hot bath, a massage with oil of soothing herbs rubbed into her skin – but no. There was work yet to be done, and she alone could do it.

Meryet turned toward her husband's chambers. Inside, Meryet found that Thutmose had set an untouched tray piled with figs, roasted fish, and discs of golden bread on the bright tiles of his floor. Instead of his mid-day meal, a scattering of maps and scrolls lay strewn across the ebony-wood table. Baubles from the Pharaoh's apartment held curls of papyrus open: a silver drinking cup, a dagger in a turquoise sheath, a fist-sized scarab of chipped blue lapis, carved on its flat underside with some tidbit of news or other – the birth of a new child into a noble house, a wedding, a funeral. Thutmose hunched over his scrolls, tracing a line on a map. The slide of his finger over the papyrus hissed softly like a snake moving through river reeds. He glanced up at her through the fringe of his wig and smiled, but did not straighten from his work.

Meryet made her way to Thutmose's side, sank onto his silk-covered couch to rest her head against his strong shoulder.

"Trouble in Kadesh," Thutmose muttered.

"There is always trouble in Kadesh."

"More trouble than usual this time, I think. The raids are worse than any I've read about in previous years. More raiders, too. Kadesh is riling itself for war – a greater war than it's yet attempted."

Meryet said nothing. She knew he liked to talk his plans over, to pour his thoughts into her like wine into a cup, so he might taste their merit on his own tongue. More would be forthcoming.

"My forces are already spread too thin. Kush is finally subdued, I think, but Mitanni has been so demanding this past year. And there have been disturbing reports from the Delta. The Sea People are marauding again. They are not in the Delta – not yet. But they will make their way south, and they *will* strike. It's a matter of when, not if. But Kadesh – that's my most immediate concern. Hatshepsut and I have worked hard to install fortresses near their border, and no doubt they've realized we plan to push Egypt's boundaries across their own. But I may have underestimated their response."

"What is your plan, then?"

Thutmose sighed. He rested his cheek on the crown of her head, finally tearing his eyes from the scrolls. "I don't have one. Yet. I ought to speak with Hatshepsut, but..."

"Now is not the time, Thutmose."

"I know."

Meryet left the couch, paced across the expanse of his chamber to examine the gleaming statues of the gods set into their little alcoves. She stared pensively at their small faces and felt the same strange mixture of embarrassment and dread she always felt when she looked at a god. Their eyes were always so distant, so unseeing. And yet they smiled at her, small, almost secretive smiles, as if they saw her plainly and were amused by the futility of her mortal efforts and fears. *If a Pharaoh is the next thing to divine, then why do I never see Thutmose smile this way? Why are gods free of cares, but not a king – or his Great Royal Wife?*

As she turned back to her husband, she caught her own reflection in his wall mirror, a wide expanse of electrum polished to a flawless silver glow. The startling youth of her image arrested her for a moment, and she stared, disbelieving. This round, smooth, unlined face could not be what her subjects saw – could it? She felt the weight of her cares dragging at her, and yet she stood easily, gracefully erect, moved with a freedom her ka did not feel. Even her breasts were round and firm, having recovered from Amunhotep's birth as only a very young woman's body may do. In the mirror's reflection she watched Thutmose turn back to his scrolls, and the smooth boyishness of his hands, the faint suggestion of childhood plumpness still rounding his cheeks, nearly made her laugh aloud.

We are barely more than children, she thought, *and half divine. With all the weight of responsibility on us. And somehow it does not show.*

"Thutmose," she said, "I have never seen such grief before."

He sat back, turned his full attention upon Meryet. "Hatshepsut?"

"When will it be time to tell her the truth?"

Thutmose sighed. "I don't know."

"She knows Senenmut was murdered. Once her grief is not so fresh, she will want to know who killed him, and why.

She will want his killer brought to justice."

"*Will* she want that, once she knows the truth?"

Meryet considered. At last she said, "I don't know. But I do know that she must be told. It is maat."

"You are right, of course." He held out his arms to her, and gratefully, she went to him. She settled against his side, tucked her face against his neck to breathe in his scent, a rich, earthy smell of horses, harness leather, the offering smoke of the temples. "I fear telling her, you know," Thutmose went on. "I fear how she will react. What she might choose to do."

"And yet it is a choice *she* must make, whether to seek justice or not."

"I fear she will blame me."

"You are not to blame."

"I'm not so certain of that." He flipped a sandaled foot at his table, and his toe caught the edge of a scroll. The papyrus sheets whispered together like dry leaves on a winter sycamore. "I'm not certain of anything just now."

"I am certain of you," Meryet said, twining her arms around his waist, holding him tight.

"I wish I shared that certainty."

"You must tell her soon, Thutmose. Let her do all her grieving at once."

He paused, and in the silence she felt his hesitation. She bit her lip, willed him to see the sense of it, willed him to see maat.

Then she felt the tension leave his body. She felt his back stoop a little as he assumed yet another of the gods' burdens.

"I will," he promised. "I will tell her everything I know when she is ready to see me. When she summons me, I'll tell her."

CHAPTER TWO

F OR TWO WEEKS THE SECOND throne on the Pharaohs' dais stood empty, and Thutmose held court alone. He knew himself to be a capable young man, equal to the task of shouldering the burden without his partner-king beside him. All the same, he missed Hatshepsut, for her presence in the throne room had become as routine to him as watching the sun rise in the eastern sky. The starkness of her vacant seat left a heaviness in his chest that dulled his wits and plagued him with a constant nervous tension, so that when her fan-bearer Batiret finally appeared one evening requesting his presence in Hatshepsut's garden, the relief of seeing her again was almost greater than his guilt and worry.

He went to her at once, allowing Batiret to lead him in silence through the dim night-time corridors of the palace toward Hatshepsut's wing. Her apartments, usually lively with the sound of her women spinning flax and laughing, or ringing with the performances of her musicians, stood silent and blue in the cooling air. When the two great doors of Hatshepsut's chambers materialized out of the darkness, carved with scarabs, their gilded surface quietly alive with a night-dampened shine, Batiret slowed and crept forward as hesitant as a mouse. In the eloquence of the silence that greeted him, Thutmose understood that the past two weeks had been a time of unrelenting mourning for the woman he loved as a mother. Sour guilt curdled in his heart.

He made his way to her garden, feet dragging on her

cold, quiet floors. Servants clustered near the door to her chambers, hanging back, reluctant to approach their mistress unless commanded. He moved out alone into the foreign coolness of Hatshepsut's garden, borne on a current of maat, helpless to stop his own drifting. The night had turned everything within the high walls to a curious shade of blue-green, the color of a turquoise stone plunged into deep water. The sameness of color made his head swim. He felt he moved through the veils of a dream.

He found her crouched on a stone bench beneath a little stand of myrrh trees. The odor of their sap burned his nostrils with their sweetness. Hatshepsut's shoulders sagged; her hands lay listless on her knees. She did not look up at him when he lowered himself to the bench at her side.

Thutmose had practiced what he would say to her dozens of times, but now, confronted with the dullness of her sorrow and the fierce burning of his own self-loathing, he found all his rehearsed words had withered on his tongue. He sat in silence, listening to the calls of insects in the flower beds, a sound as monotonous and soothing as the endless rolling of a chariot's wheels.

At last he said, "Lately I have felt many regrets, Hatshepsut. I regret the thing I made you do – sending him away. I thought it was maat, but now I am not certain. Now that I know what true companionship is – what I have with Meryet – now I feel evil for having caused you such pain."

She shifted a little, but said nothing. Still, in her small response he sensed her acceptance. She did not forgive him, and he deserved no forgiveness. But she accepted the rough, heartfelt offering of his words.

It was time. Thutmose drew a ragged breath, stared out into the garden's deep blue-green. He knew his words would shatter whatever peace she had managed to find in the time since Senenmut's death, and whatever small comfort she took from his apology. He knew, too, that Meryet was right, that Hatshepsut's kas could not heal their grave wounds until she knew the truth.

"Mawat...Nehesi and I have reason to believe that it was Neferure who killed Senenmut."

For one hopeful heartbeat the garden remained still, and Thutmose thought wildly that perhaps she already knew – perhaps she had already grieved for this, too. Then the world seemed to contract around them, a strange sinking, sucking feeling, as if all of Egypt drew in a great breath of choking poison. Hatshepsut swayed, staggered to her feet like a puppet in a marketplace show, her body pulled inexorably upward by an unseen hand on an unbreakable cord. Her mouth opened, and Thutmose braced for the agony of her scream. Instead, only a short, low wail came from her chest, thin, almost musical. It pierced deep into his heart.

She crumpled onto the grass. Thutmose saw, from the tail of his eye, her women rush forward. They stopped when he held up a hand; they milled in the shadows like restless horses their bodies colliding and rebounding, their hands flying like startled birds.

Thutmose knelt beside the king. Already a layer of dew had sprung up on the grass. It soaked the hem of his kilt; a chill crept into his skin. He took Hatshepsut's shoulders in his hands, tried to lift her from the wet grass, but her grief pinioned her to the earth, and he was as helpless to raise her as he would be to lift an obelisk into the sky.

"I curse you," Hatshepsut keened against the earth, her voiced high and ragged with pain. Thutmose's heart quailed under the curse, but she spoke on, and he realized her hatred was not for him. "Mut, Khonsu, Iset, Sobek! All the gods! Amun, I curse you! Hathor, I curse you – I curse you!"

What could he do but kneel beside her? Her head lolled from side to side, face down against the grass. When her sobs grew less frequent, Thutmose took her in his hands again, and this time he could lift her to rest her wet cheek against his neck. The stained tunic she wore was soaked through with dew and tears; she shivered in the night breeze. Thutmose wrapped his arms tightly around her shaking body.

"I remember," he said quietly, close to her ear, "standing in a field of emmer at the Festival of Min. Do you recall? That year with the bull...." He bit his tongue. Better not to remind her of Neferure now. "I remember looking up at you, at how fine and strong you looked in the white crown. I was just a boy. I thought I would never live up to your strength. I am just a boy still, Mawat. But you have the same strength inside you. I know you do."

"It is gone," Hatshesput moaned. "Drained away."

"Never. You still live. You are still the king."

Moving as stiffly as a crone, she extracted herself from Thutmose's arms. Hatshepsut climbed to her feet, hobbled down the blue-green path to stand facing away from him, gazing high and far beyond the top of the garden wall.

He went to her, stared out into the night in the direction of her stare, but saw nothing at first. Then he realized that two stars burned brighter and larger than the rest, and with a warmer hue. They rode low in the northern sky, barely clearing the violet line of the wall. No – they were not stars, but moonlight reflecting from the golden capstones of the two obelisks at Ipet-Isut.

"That is where I live," she said dully, "there, and nowhere else. Only in stone. Only in memory. The breath of life has gone out of me."

"No, Mawat."

She turned to stare into his face. The sudden intensity of her eyes pushed him backward. For a moment he thought foolishly of fleeing. But he was the king, as surely as she, and a king ran from neither his fears nor his loves.

"Gods, Thutmose. *You* have regrets? They are nothing beside mine. I spent so much time fretting over others taking my throne from me – taking all I loved from me. In the end, it was I who took it all. I stole it from myself. I robbed my own heart. I clung so tightly to what didn't matter, and I lost everything that did. Everything. You cannot imagine how bitter it tastes. Do not make the same mistake, Thutmose. No gilded chair or palace is worth this loss, no temple, no crown. Promise me you won't sacrifice everything. Not everything."

Thutmose swallowed hard. His eyes burned; he rubbed them hard with his fists. His ka was not so certain that the throne was not worth sacrifice. The Horus Throne was the legacy of their family; it their unbreakable link to all who had come before, and to all who would come after for generations unending. It was their blood, their bones, their kas. He thought of Amunhotep, warm and safe and growing in the nursery. He thought of grandchildren to come, all of them inheriting the divinity and the power that was his to give. He tasted Hatshepsut's bitterness, but felt, too, his own determination rise like a cobra from the sand.

But Hatshepsut was staring at him, expectant, her eyes alight with the fire of her urgency. She seized him by the shoulders with hands suddenly as strong as a hawk's talons, and he quailed under the hardness of her grip. "Promise me, Thutmose. Tell me you will not choose the throne over the things that truly matter – over family, over love. Over eternity."

"I promise, Mawat. I promise."

CHAPTER THREE

SATIAH LOWERED THE BAG OF incense outside the High Priest's door. She sighed gratefully, stretching her back, shaking a cramp from her thigh. The sack weighed nearly as much as she, and toting it from the storeroom to the High Priest's chamber had taken her longer than it would have taken a strong young man. But the chore was an opportunity to demonstrate her dedication. Satiah never missed such an opportunity, if the gods would allow it. Of course, it was not dedication to the High Priest that concerned her. In the end, he was but a man, and men were impermanent. It was the god she hoped to impress. Ah, that was her goal in all things.

She clapped, and after a long moment the door creaked opened. Tenry, High Priest of Min in the city of Abedju, was as kind a man as Satiah had ever met. He was barely clinging to the last threads of middle age, and his shameful mortality had begun to show plainly in the deep lines of his face and the gray wisps of hair that sometimes poked from beneath his wig when he had grown careless with his appearance. He stood at his doorway now with one side of his face rather puffy and red, an obvious sign that he had given in to an old man's weariness and stolen a nap when all the god's servants, even the highest, should have been hard at work.

I mustn't judge him, Satiah reminded herself. *It is not his fault he's mortal. True divinity is given to few — only the most devout, the most pure.*

"Ah," Tenry said. "Incense for tomorrow's offerings." He chuckled as he assessed the weight of the sack. "Tomorrow's and much more. What a diligent priestess. Min blesses us in you, little Satiah."

She allowed her cheeks to color, and looked shyly down at her toes.

"It is past time for the mid-day meal. Have you eaten yet, child?"

"No, High Priest. I have been working."

"Won't you share some bread and beer with me? I would be grateful for the chance to get to know you better. One of my newest priestesses, and yet the hardest-working. You must have had a remarkable life, remarkable parents, to raise such an obedient and dutiful daughter."

"You are kind, but I have so many chores to see to."

"Well," Tenry said, "it is true that a priest's work is never done. Or a priestess's work, I suppose. Very well; we will talk some other time, when we both have more leisure. You won't forget to take some leisure now and then, will you? It is good for the heart and the ka. Here, take some bread and cheese with you. No, I insist. A little wisp of smoke like you needs all the bread she can get."

Satiah took the food with a nod of thanks and turned back to her duties. The door shut softly behind her, accompanied by another of Tenry's fond chuckles. She sped back toward the storerooms, and when she rounded a bend in the temple's corridor she pressed herself into the shadow of a recessed doorway and ate the crumbling bread and hard cheese in a few bites. The bread stuck painfully in her throat; she gulped at it, eyes watering, until at last it settled into her hollow stomach.

She was thinner than ever now, for though she received ample vouchers for bread and beer, the usual payment for an apprentice priestess, as well as a share of Abedju's offerings of fruit and cheese, meat and honey cakes, most of what she earned as a priestess was paid out again. She cashed only enough of her vouchers at the city's storehouses to keep herself alive and strong enough to do her work – not enough to get plump and indolent like the other priestesses of Min. No – she needed her earnings. Satiah had expenses that must not be neglected. She had a duty to the gods. She checked the yellow belt cinching her rough-spun linen tunic. The week's vouchers were still safely tucked away in the folds of its fabric.

The bread and cheese dulled the familiar, pervasive gnawing of her belly. She stretched her arms above her head, humming a happy tune. There were indeed duties yet to attend. She had not simply thrown Tenry off the subject of her family and history out of habit, though the gods knew she had become adept at polite deflections and quick to dodge the kind inquiries of priests at temples all along the course of the Iteru. No, there were offerings of gold and precious stones to weigh and sort, and somebody had to oversee the washing. The tunics of the servants of Min would never stay gleaming white on their own.

Satiah smiled at the prospect of a full day still laying ahead. Work was good. Work made her happy, filled her with a deep satisfaction at the setting of the sun, a sensation she had come to appreciate as she had lain on the creaking wicker couch in Harit's hut night after night, those many months ago. She had loved weeding the dark rows of the fields, plunging her hands into the damp coolness of moist earth, though her back cramped from the stooping. She had loved hauling water for the goats, milking them, pressing her face against their bristly sides and giggling at the sounds their wide bellies made while her hands coaxed frothing milk from warm udders. She had grieved when she'd realized it was time to move on from Harit's farm, but Waset was too near, and Satiah could never rest easily at night, knowing that the palace was only a bowshot away. Satiah had work to do even then, duties to fulfill. Her old life was a threat to her new and precious obligations, and so the very city itself was a threat.

When she knew the time had come to leave, she had slipped a sharp knife from Harit's small, humble kitchen, tucked it into her belt, and made her way north toward Senenmut's estate. From there, her new life had begun, and Satiah had never before known such joy. With her family's sins atoned for and the taint in her blood washed clean, the gods had given her what she had longed for. At last.

In the alcove behind the Room of Offerings, Satiah worked with her fellow priestesses to organize the tangle of gold chains, the hoops of copper bracelets, the unset cabochons of glimmering stones. They packed each type of treasure into flat cedar chests between layers of linen while Satiah led them in song after song to lighten their hearts as they bent to the task. By the time the evening bell sounded, a clangor that rang rhythmically through the corridors and courtyards of the Temple of Min, her crew of workers were wiping sweat from their brows but could not chase the grins from their faces.

"Satiah," Tuya said, laughing, "you know how to make the most dreary task go by in a wink." She threw her arms around Satiah, who returned the warm embrace. "I don't know how we got along here before you came stumbling through the temple gate with your feet blistered and swollen."

"By Min," said Iset-Weret, an older priestess with a voice as rich and soft as smoke, "our little Satiah has blossomed like a flower in the sun. It won't be long before she's High Priestess, I wager."

"Not I." Satiah waved away their praises with frantic hands. "I'm not worthy!"

"Pah! There's never been a worthier woman. Come share some wine with us tonight. We'll have a game of senet."

"You're kind," Satiah said, "but I must get to bed early tonight."

"Another early morning for the little buzzing bee. Very

well, then. Sleep soundly, child. When you're High Priestess you can send us all to bed early without our wine and senet."

It might make them more dedicated workers, she mused, before she could dismiss the unworthy thought.

High Priestess. She considered the peace she had here in Abedju. Since leaving Harit and Baki, she had worked her way from temple to temple, walking from one town to the next, living off what she could earn as a priestess and the occasional kindness of strangers. The only temples she avoided were Hathor's. Though it pained her to keep far from the Lady's side, she knew where Hatshepsut's eyes and ears would be, and so she served instead at the houses of lesser gods. They were lesser compared to the Lady's brilliance, but ah, still divine. They were the best times she had ever known, those days of free movement, living off her wits and her charm, maintaining a near-constant state of rapturous communion with the gods. But High Priestess – such an assignment would require her to put down roots, to remain in Abedju. It would be an honor, but a vanishingly small one compared to the great honor the gods had given her already. She needed nothing else. She had the ultimate proof of her devotion, proof of a sanctity no High Priestess could ever hope to achieve.

Satiah made her way through the quiet corridors as the sun sank red across the wide, gleaming expanse of the Iteru. The evening air was dusty and calm, and filled her lungs with its spicy-dry taste, a satisfaction that was nearly deep enough to quell the hunger that returned to plague her belly. She pressed her hand against her sash once more and heard the grain vouchers crinkle reassuringly.

She reached the door to her tiny chamber at last, pushed it open on squealing hinges. Besu bent over the small, narrow bed, her broad back to Satiah as she worked. A small bronze lamp was already burning on the rickety table in the corner. Beneath the table was the tiny, dark-oiled cedar chest containing all of Satiah's belongings: the only furniture the room could hold.

Besu straightened, lifted the freshly swaddled babe to her shoulder. When the boy saw Satiah, he smiled his pink, toothless grin.

"Give him here," she said, and Besu handed him over gently. Beneath her cheap linen dress, the woman's breasts swung heavy with milk. Satiah pinched the baby's fat little elbow, smiling in satisfaction. He was growing well, getting strong, though he was small for his age, she knew. She kissed him on his plump, rosy cheek. "Mawat missed her little prince, yes she did."

She laid Amenemhat carefully on the bed, where he fussed in his crackly voice. Satiah drew the vouchers from her sash and counted them carefully, subtracted her small share, and handed the remainder to Besu.

"Thank you, Lady Satiah."

Satiah smiled in spite of the hollow pain in her middle. She thought longingly of the bread and cheese she'd had at mid-day, pushed the thought away again roughly. *It does you no good to dwell on your hunger. The gods will provide. They always do.*

"There is a jar of goat's milk for him there on the table, for his night feedings."

"Good. You have done well, Besu, as always. The gods blessed me when I found you."

"I've...I've taken the liberty of bringing you some honey cakes from home, Lady Satiah. I hope I didn't overstep...."

Satiah laughed with pleasure. "You are so kind. I am grateful. I'll see you in the morning."

Besu took her leave, and Satiah unwrapped the bit of oiled linen to expose the cold, sticky cakes. She at them slowly, savoring the sweetness and the coarse graininess of the crumbs. She lay on her narrow bed with her son propped against her chest, and felt the cadence of her heart thrumming through his tiny body, echoing along his small, plump limbs.

"Son of the gods," she whispered, and kissed the top of his warm, soft head. "Son of all the gods. One day we will make our way home, and then, I promise you, the throne will be yours."

The taste of that certainty was sweeter than the honey.

Chapter Four

O R AT LEAST, THAT'S WHAT his nurses tell me." Meryet set her wine cup back on the table. It clicked faintly against the polished ebony wood, and at the sound, Thutmose's eyes snapped out of their unfocused blear. He stared at the cup; the sharpness of its details shocked him, the brilliance of the blue scarabs dancing around its rim leaping forward with accusing ferocity. He had been staring into the distance, had hardly heard a word of his wife's conversation. He struggled to recall, through his fog of vague worry, what Meryet had been saying.

"Er...standing already? That boy's a strong one."

Meryet frowned at him. "I told you he's standing minutes ago, Thutmose. I was speaking of his words. He will begin talking soon – real words – that's what the nurses say. It's early, for both standing and talking. He is blessed by the gods." She said this last with the annoyed air of having repeated herself.

Thutmose passed a hand across his face as if he might wipe the tension away. "I'm sorry, Meryet. I didn't mean to let my thoughts wander. We rarely spend time together these days, I've been so preoccupied. I do want to hear all your news."

They paused awkwardly while the servants entered with the supper trays. A fragrant roast of goose, sprouting a tail of herbs singed from the clay oven, steamed on a golden platter. Bowls of sauces and stewed fruits joined it, and long, thick cores of lettuce drizzled with spiced honey – a dish appropriate for an evening of lovemaking, with its well-known ability to enflame the desires. Thutmose stared mournfully at the lettuce. He was so weary he doubted he could manage to undress his wife, never mind give a more taxing performance.

When the servants withdrew again, Meryet leaned in to slice a portion of the goose. "It's Kadesh, isn't it?"

"What's that, now?"

"Kadesh. It's why you're so distracted." She laid the meat in his bowl, ladled a thick red sauce over the pale flesh. She did not look up at him.

"Yes," he admitted with a sigh. "Amun's eyes, Meryet, the scrolls keep coming, and it gets worse all the time."

"It can't be as bad as you think."

"It may be worse than I think."

"Read a scroll to me. Let me hear it for myself." She sounded practical, business-like as she chose the plumpest stewed fruits for Thutmose's bowl.

She was so unflappable, this Great Royal Wife who was hardly more than a girl. Not for the first time, Thutmose wondered what good deed he had ever done, that the gods had seen fit to reward him with Meryet. She was thoughtful, confident, wiser than a priestess and stronger than a desert lioness – in her ka, if not in her rather slender body. *An improvement over my previous wife, and no mistake*, he thought as he rummaged through the basket of scrolls beside his couch.

"This one is from one of my agents in Damas: 'My sources in Kadesh tell me that King Niqmad has been in close contact with Huzziya, King of Hatti. They have seen Hittite soldiers drilling with Kadeshi soldiers, and more Hittite troops arrive every day. Multiple men have confirmed this.'" Thutmose laid that scroll aside. "Here's another from Damas: 'Word from the city of Tadmor is that recruiters came to speak to the young men of the area. They flew both Hittite and Kadeshi banners.' One from Katna: 'King Huzziya of Hatti paid triple the usual price for strong horses. He said they were to be taken to Kadesh.' From Ugarit: 'A large contingent of troops from Ebla and Alep were noted moving south toward Kadesh, under the banners of King Huzziya of Hatti along with the banners of their own city-states.'" Thutmose tossed the scrolls aside in disgust.

Meryet sat very still, her hands folded neatly in her lap. Her fine, red-painted mouth pressed into a tight line.

"So?" said Thutmose.

"Kadesh, Tadmor, Ebla, Alep – all Retjenu city-states, and all of them under the influence of Hatti."

"Yes."

Her mouth twisted as she chewed her own cheek in thought. "I suppose Damas's city-king is allied with Huzziya of Hatti, too."

"If he's not now, he soon will be."

"Your grandfather's fortress at Ugarit..."

"Is Egypt's only real stronghold in Retjenu. Kadesh and Damas are the only major cities between Egypt and Ugarit. If Huzziya thinks to cut Ugarit off from Egypt, the way to do it is to ally with Kadesh and Damas."

"If Egypt is cut off from Ugarit, much trade will be lost."

"I know," he said. "It would be too great a blow. It would set the Two Lands back to where we stood in the days of King Ahmose."

"Or back further still. To the days when the Heqa-Khasewet ruled."

"Never. I won't allow it to come to that."

"And yet that is precisely what Huzziya and this Niqmad of Kadesh are planning: a gradual takeover. And an invasion of the northern sepats, once they've gathered enough city-states to make an attempt on Egypt's borders. You see that, surely."

"Of course."

Meryet clenched her fists against the fine, soft linen of her gown. "Hatshepsut saved Retjenu from starvation. And here they are, plotting with the Hittites. Are their memories so short?"

Thutmose waved a hand as if shooing away flies. "The Retjenu live in tents – most of them, those who aren't in the cities. Their men lie with ewes; they tile their floors with sheep shit. They can hardly be called civilized. Surely you don't expect men like the Retjenu to remember that the Pharaoh saved them from famine. Not when Huzziya comes waving his banners and talking of bringing Egypt to its knees. No doubt he's promised Retjenu a tribute of Egyptian grain if they'll help put him on the Horus Throne."

"Hatti is very powerful, Thutmose. I know this; I grew up in the north. Hatti was never far from anyone's thoughts in my father's house."

"Until these reports came in, I thought Huzziya was content with our alliance."

"Hittites are never content with anything. They have always been Egypt's most dangerous enemy, even when they've played at honoring an alliance."

"If they get a toehold in Kadesh..."

"They'll cut you off from your forces in Ugarit. Not for long; not permanently. But it will give them enough time to swarm over our northeastern border and take Lower Egypt, or at least damage it."

"You're right. I know you're right."

"You should sail for the north, Thutmose. Take two-thirds of your troops and move them to Lower Egypt."

"I can send them, but..."

"You must go yourself. The gods know I don't want you so far from my side – you know that. But your men need to see you at their head, and more than that, Hatti and Retjenu must know that a young, strong, *male* king is at their border. They will not respect anything else. I know the way their thoughts run."

"And that's the trouble. Hatshepsut. She's still out of sorts. I've hardly seen her in weeks. She avoids her throne, avoids ruling. How can I leave Egypt in her hands, when she is so broken?"

"You still feel guilt."

"I will always feel guilt."

Meryet laid her hand on his thigh, then lifted his arm and tucked herself beneath it. He felt her warmth against his skin. The perfumed strands of her wig brushed his chest, filling his senses with her heady, womanly scent. "You cannot shoulder this guilt forever, Thutmose."

"It is my guilt, and I *can* shoulder it forever. I will. I wronged her, and now she suffers."

"Trust the Horus Throne to me. Let Hatshepsut mourn, and allow me to command from the throne in your place while you're gone. You know I'll do the job well."

"I know."

"And you know I'm right, that you must go north."

He sighed heavily. "I just can't leave her, Meryet. I fear for her. She's...she's the only mother I've ever known. It pains me to see her so broken."

"You cannot mend her, Thutmose. Not by staying here. You can't mend her, but you can prevent Egypt from shattering."

He pulled her closer, pressing her against his flesh as if he might, by sheer force of will, make their two bodies into one, the way a potter makes a single strong vessel from two slabs of clay. Perhaps then her strength would be his. But he said nothing, gave no promise, made no commitments.

Meryet pulled away from him. Reluctantly, he loosened his grip.

"Listen, Pharaoh of Egypt." She trailed one finger playfully across his lower lip. "You have been working too hard. You need time away from Waset."

"There's no time to take."

"I don't suggest you go off on a hunt. A pilgrimage – that's what you need. Get away from your throne for a few days. Get away from Ipet-Isut, too. Go and commune with the gods in peace. Ask them what you must do. They will answer."

"A pilgrimage." He weighed the thought in his heart.

"Visit temples. I don't care whether you sail north or south. The gods are the same wherever you go. Spend some time in smaller towns, in more pleasant settings than Waset. Take a few men with you, and go clear your heart of all these doubts and fears. I will tend the throne while you're gone, and perhaps you will see that I'm capable of ruling in your absence – and Hatshepsut's absence."

Thutmose nodded. "If it was just for a short time, perhaps...."

"It's a good plan."

He almost nodded his consent, but a sudden memory returned to him, the vision sharp and obscenely colorful in his heart's eye. He recalled Neferure standing in her little palace with the knife in her hand, the fan-bearer's blood running from the tip of the blade, as brilliantly red as a sunset. He did not believe Neferure was dead. She was out there somewhere, haunting the Two Lands like an ill spirit, and she was quite capable of doing to Meryet what she had done to Senenmut.

"I'll take a pilgrimage," Thutmose said, "on one condition. Take Hatshepsut's guardsman into your own service for as long as I am gone."

"Nehesi?" Meryet tilted her head in bewilderment. "Why?"

"If I can't be at your side, I want him there."

Meryet shrugged. "Very well. I will take him for my own guard, if Hatshepsut will let him go."

"She will. She'll do it for you. She'll do it if I tell...if I suggest it."

"Then it's settled," Meryet said. She rose smoothly from the couch. "Supper's gone cold, but it doesn't matter. I'm hungry for something else now." She took his hand and led him to his own bed chamber. When she closed the door and smiled up at him, her eyes dark as smoke and intense as stars, Thutmose found he was wakeful enough to do more than undress her, after all.

Chapter Five

THUTMOSE ALLOWED THE REINS TO slide through his hands. His pair of horses, black as deep water, lowered their heads gratefully as they relaxed into a walk. Their backs dished with each step, an easy, fluid motion. White patches of frothy sweat dried on their withers and flanks, but their breathing was calm now, and they paced slowly, confidently, back toward Abedju. Behind him, a few more chariots trailed across the hills, dry in the late Shemu heat. His men had gathered up the gazelle and hares they had shot at the desert's edge. Tonight they would open casks of wine and feast in the house of the noble who was honored to host the king.

Meryet had been wise, as ever, to suggest the pilgrimage. Thutmose had sailed from Waset a week before, landing at each city north along the Iteru. He spent contemplative hours alone in the dim hearts of every temple he found. A certain undeniable peace came from long, quiet prayer, from burning earnest and humble offerings. These rural offerings were a far cry from those he made at the great cosmopolitan complex of Ipet-Isut. Beyond Waset's bustling reach, the small-town gods required not sacrificial bulls, but scraps of meat; not casks of well-aged wine poured like a red river along well-washed paving stones, but cups of sweet milk laid out at the gods' feet. Here, worship was less spectacular by far, yet the thin streams of smoke that rose from his offering bowls buoyed his hopes and cleared his heart of doubt as no ceremonial pomp ever could.

Beside him in the chariot, his favorite scribe Tjaneni raised a hand to shield his eyes against the sun's glare. The heat of the day beat upon Thutmose's skin, soaked into his shoulders and forearms. The strength of Re's light was an encouragement.

"A good hunt, Mighty Horus," Tjaneni said. "Your aim is enough to make Set envious."

"You are no slouch with the bow yourself, Tjaneni."

The scribe shrugged. "I come from a long line of hunters. It's in our blood."

"Then you won't mind coming along with me to Kadesh. You can fire your bow at traitors instead of gazelle."

Tjaneni raised one thick eyebrow. "So you are going to Kadesh, then?"

"I don't see that I have a choice." In spite of his words, he said them with confidence. His week of prayer had soothed his ka with peace. He felt steady as a deep-hulled barque, the kind that cuts through Iteru waves like a hot knife through beeswax.

"Well," Tjaneni said lightly, "Kadeshis can't leap as high or run as fast as gazelle. They must be easier targets."

Thutmose chuckled. "If I wait too long, it will be impossible to stop their treachery with Hatti. Better to cull the gazelle herd now, before the disease spreads."

"I eagerly await the hunt, Majesty."

They rolled through the outskirts of Abedju, Thutmose raising his hand now and then to acknowledge the rekhet shouts of acclaim. The dirt lanes between small huts gave way to larger roads, hard-packed and rutted by generations of wheels. Two-story mudbrick houses rose on either side, their roofs crowned by bright cloth sunshades where the wives of merchants and craftsmen did their spinning and weaving, weathering the worst of the summer heat where a cool wind might lift sweat from a sun-darkened brow. The road wended past a covered well. Women clustered about the stone cistern, gossiping as they hauled buckets hand over hand. As Thutmose passed, a few let go their ropes to bow; the buckets splashing back into the cool depths raised a scent of mineral dampness on the air.

Beyond a bend in the road, the pylons of a temple gate rose above a colorful canopy of sunshades that rippled like river water in the rising evening breeze.

"Whose temple is that, Tjaneni?"

Tjaneni squinted. "Min's, I believe, Horus."

"I haven't visited it yet, have I?"

"Not Min's – not here in Abedju."

Thutmose sent his men and the day's game on to the fine estate of the noble who hosted them. "I owe Min a visit," he said. "When I catch up with you I expect to smell that gazelle roasting, eh?"

In the forecourt, Thutmose maneuvered his chariot through a crowd of bowing priests. Two rows of raised water gardens lined the avenue to the temple's steps. Lotuses bloomed in the turquoise pools, vivid purple, wreathing the air with their intoxicating perfume. Clouds of gnats spun above the sweet flowers, and now and then a bird dived among the insects with a soft rush of feathers. Thutmose felt the deep peace of divinity beckon, drawing him toward the heart of the god's great sanctuary, where Min's blessing and reassurance would be added to those already gifted to his heart by so many other generous and benevolent gods.

He left Tjaneni holding the reins and walked alone up the pale sandstone steps into the temple. The coolness of indoor shade closed abruptly over his head. He inhaled deeply the sharp-sweet odor of ages of burnt resin. Two priestesses bowed at his elbow, young women near his own age. They were dressed simply in the white tunic and yellow sash of their god and office. The pretty modesty of their appearance seemed just another of Abedju's rustic delights. One priestess furnished him with an ornate bronze bowl for his offerings. The other plucked a few red coals from a nearby brazier with her blackened tongs. Thutmose carried his bowl carefully toward the double doors of Min's private chamber. The heat of it soaked through the thick wool pad that protected his hands. His palms tingled.

He never knew what caused him to glance to his right in that moment just before a priest opened the door to the god's sanctuary. Some small movement, a brush of bright white linen against the temple's inner shadow. He saw a girl moving rapidly from one doorway to another, face turned down to the floor. She was dressed in the simple tunic and yellow sash of a Min priestess. Young, pretty, small of stature and thin as a copper needle, she moved with a curious, graceful fluidity that was somehow laced with inborn arrogance.

Thutmose froze. He stared at the place where the girl had vanished into the black mouth of a doorway. His heart climbed high in his chest, beating wildly, a tight pain in his throat.

"Great Lord? Is aught amiss?" One of the priestesses was at his side. He turned to her without answer and deposited the bronze bowl with its wool pad in her startled hands. Then he hurried down the hallway after the girl.

Shadows rose up around him as he drew further from the brazier-lit antechamber. The sudden arches of black doorways yawned in darkened walls. Niches like staring eyes appeared and seemed to blink as he passed, closing over the dully glimmering statues of Min that waited in each with silent expectation.

Thutmose reached the door he thought the girl had entered, pushed his way inside. The chamber was unlit, and far too black to make out any detail. He took a tentative step forward, blundered into some heavy bulk, a stack of chests filled with offerings. A storeroom. He would find nothing in here without a light.

He withdrew into the hallway. The two priestesses stood there, eyes wide with self-conscious worry. One still held his offering bowl; the glow of its coals inside cast a sinister red light on her breasts and face, inverting her features an darkening the sockets of her eyes.

"Mighty Horus," said the other priestess, panic edging her voice, "please allow us to serve you. What do you require?"

Thutmose peered into the storeroom. The glow of the offering dish was not enough to light even an arm's length of the room. There was nothing to see, nothing to hear. And yet he had been *sure*.

"Nothing," he managed. "Nothing, good ladies. I thought... but never mind. Please, show me into Min's sanctuary."

As he knelt before the god, slipping bits of dried meat from the traveling pouch at his belt and dropping them onto the red embers, a terrible cold settled into Thutmose's heart. He might be mistaken. He prayed that he was. And yet he had recognized Neferure in that brief instant as she crossed the hall. Thutmose was certain it had been she.

When his offerings to Min were gone, the smoke of his fire dispersing into the haze of incense clouding the chamber, Thutmose crept from the temple and back to his chariot. The peace he had found in his week of contemplation and prayer seemed to rock and quiver, like a fragile egg rolling round the edge of its nest, teetering above sharp rocks far below.

CHAPTER SIX

THUTMOSE WOKE WELL BEFORE DAWN. In truth, he was unsure whether he had slept at all. The night had passed in fitful cycles of restless dozing and uncomfortable half-dreams, wherein he saw, wide awake and with his ka fully housed in his body, Neferure materialize out of the night-time gloom of his host's estate. She would walk toward him while he lay paralyzed on the sleeping couch, raise a dagger over her expressionless face, and vanish the moment he managed to blink his eyes or draw a ragged breath. It had been a terrible night. Thutmose was not sorry to leave it behind.

Leaving his men behind was another matter. He had not chosen his guards for their sluggish senses. He tied on a plain hunting kilt and slid one of his soldiers' unremarkable wigs from beneath a pile of linen, but even that slight rustle brought all the men to wakefulness. He was the Pharaoh, but they were men dedicated to their duty, and their duty was to keep the Pharaoh safe. He could not convince them to stay put while he ventured out into the pre-dawn grayness of Abedju alone – could not convince them short of threatening to strike off their heads for disobedience. Thutmose could never make such a threat. He'd be compelled to follow through with it, and he would not condemn good men for having the audacity to do their work and do it well. And so in the end he agreed to take three men with him: Tjaneni for his sharp eyes, and the brothers Bek and Eje, each as large and powerful as old Nehesi. They dressed plainly, concealed weapons in the belts of their kilts, and set off on foot through the still-sleeping lanes.

"Where do we go, Lord?" Tjaneni murmured, careful to keep his voice low.

"Back to the Temple of Min."

"So early? The god isn't even awake yet."

Thutmose did not reply, but paced on grimly through the streets. The square tops of the temple pylons were picked out against the coal-gray sky by a string of lamps flickering below fading stars.

They arrived at the temple just as a faint tinge of blue crept along the eastern horizon. A scatter of stars still shone here and there, fading gradually from view like a school of silver fish making their slow way into deeper water. The courtyard was silent between its raised ponds, though from some hidden sanctuary the odors of fresh burning incense and charred meat drifted, thin and light, across the open ground. The servants of Min would wake soon, and would set about their business. His time was limited.

Thutmose turned to his men. "Wait here. I won't be long."

"Let us come with you, Lord," Tjaneni said.

"There is no need. I have business with the god, and then I'll return. Brace up; no harm can come to me in a temple, even if somebody were to recognize me. And anyway," he said, his hand straying to his belt, "I have my knife."

He slipped quickly down the wide, empty walkway, his eyes steady on the pillars at the temple's mouth. No one moved about the entrance to Min's sacred home. As Thutmose paused at the foot of the steps, staring up into the blackness between the pillars, he heard the staggered, hesitant calls of birds waking, a distant, sleepy music in the pale morning air. He climbed the steps with one hand resting near the hilt of his dagger.

Beyond the entryway, the braziers stood cold and unlit on their thin legs. Thutmose peered into darkness. The air inside was dense with its own silence, pressing a great weight upon his body. He shivered at the sensation.

Thutmose turned toward the hallway where he'd run the day before. He had no reason to think he would see Neferure there again, but some faint whisper in his heart hoped that if he went back to the storeroom door, the gods would work some unseen power for him, producing Neferure from the darkness the way a court magician produces a live cobra from the folds of his sash.

The storeroom was closed, the door barred. He glanced this way and that, bouncing on the balls of his feet, at a loss. A faint scraping sounded from further down the hallway, the scuffling of sandals on stone. He made his way toward the noise, trailing his fingers along the wall to guide his steps through deep shadow. He was close enough now to the source of the scuffling that he could make out the rhythm of footfalls: the stride of a person of small stature, feet dragging under the weight of a burden. Thutmose stepped carefully, slowly, lifting and placing his feet with exaggerated care, toe to heel, soundless as a cat.

His fingers found the wall's sharp corner; the hallway intersected another, and suddenly the footsteps were upon him. In a heartbeat he saw the form in white linen emerge from the darkness, stooped under the bulk of a large, rough sack. He recognized her face at once, even turned down toward the sandstone floor and half lost in dimness. Thutmose seized her arm; she yelped and dropped the sack. It clattered when it fell, and the pungent scent of raw myrrh filled the hallway.

"It is you. I knew I saw you yesterday."

She shrank away from him. "Let me go or I'll scream."

"You won't, by order of the Pharaoh."

"Thutmose."

He dragged her back down the hallway, pressed her into

the recessed doorway of the storeroom. Outside the temple, dawn had come. A cold gray light suffused the hallway, barely brightening the interior. It limned Neferure's face with a soft sheen. She was as beautiful as she had ever been, fine-featured, dark-eyed, solemn, but she was thinner, too, and her arm, fully encircled by his grip, felt wiry and strong beneath his hand. Touching her gave him a queer thrill – partly the dark compelling arousal he'd felt whenever he had taken her before, and partly the chilling presence of divinity she had always worn about her like some brilliant shawl. That air of holiness and unreasoning self-assurance was thicker than he'd remembered. Perhaps the temple magnified it. She shifted against the storeroom door, and the tense muscle of her little arm writhed like a captured snake. The strength of her body seemed to him an outward manifestation of her holy power. Almost, he released her in fear. Then he recalled that he was the Lord of the Two Lands, and he dug his fingers into her flesh until she cringed.

"I should kill you," he growled, "I know it. For what you did to Senenmut – for what you did to Hatshepsut."

She stared up at him defiantly. His insides vibrated with the sudden force of her stare, the black shimmer of her eyes leaping at him from the soft perfection of her face. He recalled, against his will, the way she had gazed up at him in the field of emmer, a little girl standing on her toes to stroke the head of a quivering white bull.

"And yet you will not," said Neferure.

"You seem very confident of that." His voice was a croak, and he cursed the dryness of his throat.

"You are too devout. You would never harm a vessel of the gods."

"Neferure…"

"My name is Satiah. Neferure is no more."

He shook her, furious and helpless before her stare. "Neferure stands before me, guilty of murder."

"Murder? Not I. I made a sacrifice."

Thutmose's grip loosened without his permission. She tugged her arm free but made no move to leave the alcove of the doorway. She stared steadily up at him, and it seemed to Thutmose's bewildered eyes that she grew in stature.

"I set a sin to rights," Neferure murmured, "and the gods blessed me for it."

"Blessed you? What are you talking about?"

"I speak of the reason why you will not kill me, brother-husband."

Thutmose blinked at her.

"Come with me," she said. "I will show you now."

With his hand on the hilt of his knife, Thutmose trailed her reluctantly. She slid through the hallways of the Temple of Min, a blur of white linen against the slowly warming colors of sandstone, swift and silent as the shadow of a cloud. He held his breath as he moved in her wake. A curious buzzing filled his ears; a rushing sensation throbbed along his limbs.

Neferure stopped at the last door in a row of doors, all of them facing outward along the rear wall of the temple. The dawn light picked out the refuse of habitation scattered in the dusty soil of the temple's rear courtyard: three pots stacked one inside the other beside a door, a discarded pair of sandals beside another, a child's toy river horse lying on its side beneath a makeshift blanket of leaves. This was where the lesser priests and priestesses lived – they and their families. The dormitories.

Neferure pushed her door open, stepped into her room without looking round to see whether Thutmose followed. She was intent on whatever was inside, focused the way a woman only ever was in the presence of...*of her child*.

From the threshold, Thutmose watched Neferure lift a bundle to her shoulder. She cooed softly. A bit of blanket hung over the baby's face. Thutmose reached out – the room was small enough that he could touch the child from where he stood – and lifted the corner of the blanket away.

The baby was asleep, one fat cheek pressed against its mother's shoulder, the lips shining with wetness. Black curls of hair, soft and still fine, covered the warm head.

"His nurse will be here soon," Neferure said quietly. "I went out early to do some work while he slept. He always sleeps well. He's a perfect child. And why not? He was born of perfection."

Thutmose withdrew his hand. A low flame guttered in a dented lamp on a simple, well-used table. In the fitful light, he studied the baby's face. One baby looked much like another, but it was clear already that this child would have a sharply hooked nose and small chin, the stamp of their family line. Thutmose knew precious little of babies, but he had spent enough time with his own son to tell at a glance that this child was of an age with Amunhotep. He counted the months backward. It was possible.... But he and Neferure were both grandchildren of Thutmose the First. The mark of the Thutmosides did not necessarily come from him, the present king.

"Who is the father?"

Neferure spun to face him, hiding the baby from Thutmose's gaze. She stared up into his eyes with a directness that turned his stomach.

"You dare ask me such a thing? I am your Great Royal Wife."

"But surely you know you're not. You gave that all up when you left the palace."

"Should I have stayed imprisoned forever? I had work to do – a great work. I am not a bird, to sit singing in a cage."

"You are a murderer. That's what you are."

"I am a priestess. You understand nothing of it."

"Is the child mine?"

Neferure scowled at him. He resolved to draw out an answer with staunch silence, and scowled back twice as hard.

At last she said, "You remember the carvings on the walls of Hatshepsut's temple."

"Ah, of course."

"You remember how she came to be: Amun entering our grandfather's body, showing his guise only to Ahmose as she lay on her bed."

Thutmose peered at her through narrowed eyes. She was not angry now, but solemn, almost rapturous. She believed that a god had come to her to conceive this child, believed it down to the root of her ka. He saw that truth shining on her face.

"So a god came to you. Is that it?"

Neferure said nothing, only stared at him levelly.

"Which god, Neferure?"

"I am Satiah."

"Which god, *Satiah?*"

Her eyes stared beyond him, beyond the dusty communal courtyard to a vision far away. The solemnity of her face relaxed into a radiance of bliss. "*All* of them, brother."

Thutmose shook his head. "In a man's body? Whose?"

She came back to herself, and her eyes traveled scornfully down his own body to the belt of his kilt. "Yes. In a man's body."

Thutmose shifted under her reproachful stare. "Regardless of what you think of the child's conception, tell me, *Satiah*, why I shouldn't kill you."

"I did not say you shouldn't. I said you will not. You remember, Thutmose. I know you do. You remember the Bull of Min. You know the power I have always held within me. You know I am chosen by the gods. If you strike down a sacred vessel, you will be forever cursed – you know it's true.

And this child – Amenemhat, my son, my gift from the gods, my reward as their consort – he is the proof of my divinity."

She turned again, so Thutmose could see the sleeping babe in profile. The little nose was indeed showing signs of the same strong arch that Thutmose himself had. He stared at the boy, and he was not certain that the boy's blood was not his own. The rays of the rising sun broke free of the temple's high outer wall. They fell warm upon Thutmose's back, spilled over his shoulder. A shaft of sunlight, sparkling with drifting motes, fell across Amenemhat's face. His soft skin lit with a strange translucence. Thutmose staggered backward through the doorway. Neferure – Satiah – stepped out into the light of morning. The sun glowed on her, too, picking out her features in sharp poignancy, glimmering in the strands of her simple wig as though her braids were threaded with gold.

Thutmose heard again the bellowing of the bull, felt its thunder shake his bones. Before she could see any tremor of fear in his body, he turned on his heel and left Satiah standing there with her child. But the piercing power of her eyes followed him, taunted him, dogging his heels all the way back through the temple gates to the place where his men stood waiting for their king.

CHAPTER SEVEN

T HE FIVE FESTIVAL DAYS OF the New Year had come and gone, and with them came the Inundation. Egypt turned once more into a vast plain of water, running the length of the Iteru's long northward track, a lush, lazy wetland lying satisfied in the sun between the hills and cliffs of the eastern and western banks. The days grew redolent with the earthy perfumes of the flood. By night, the stars themselves seemed to chant the loud choruses of frogs. Akhet was a season for replenishment, for healing. It was a time to start life anew.

Meryet grunted as she lifted Amunhotep to her hip. The boy was over a year old now, and though his height was nothing for the nurses to exclaim over, he was growing stocky and strong just like his father. He was a stout little bull, though his temper was sweet as a gazelle's. Meryet kissed his fat cheeks until he squealed with laughter, held him close to her chest. She was grateful to the gods for this boy – ah, all mothers were grateful for their babes. But Amunhotep seemed imbued with a special kind of magic. As the flood waters rose, gifting their black silt to make Egypt bloom with life once more, Hatshepsut had begun to return tentatively to the world, and all because of this little boy.

"You are a golden treasure," Meryet whispered to her son. Nothing but Amunhotep could coax a smile to his grandmother's face. Nothing but holding the boy, playing with him, watching him toddle about her garden, could cause Hatshepsut to forget her many sorrows, her bitter regrets, and live instead in the moment the gods laid before her.

Meryet made her way through the Pharaoh's great apartments to the garden behind her bed chamber, trailed by her retinue of women, Amunhotep's nurse, and, of course, Nehesi. The grass beneath her sandals was wet and lush, the earth still springy with the last traces of the flood. Hatshepsut waited on a blanket in the sun, a few of Amunhotep's favorite toys scattered around her. She wore a man's kilt and a profusion of beaded necklaces, her chest and back bare. The plucky, daring nature of the garb cheered Meryet – it seemed another small sign that some fractional part of the Pharaoh's old self was returning.

"There is the little king," Hatshepsut said, smiling up at them, squinting through her kohl in the glare of the sun.

Meryet lowered Amunhotep and herself onto the blanket. The boy at once wiggled from her arms and busied himself with a wooden deby and a wool-stuffed lion. Batiret joined them, dipping cool wine from a jar, passing cups to her mistress and to Meryet.

"He grows so fast," Hatshepsut said, never taking her eyes from Amunhotep. "In a blink, he'll be as big as a horse with a deep voice and hair on his chin."

She shifted to take one of the cakes Batiret offered, but her outstretched hand arrested in the air. Hatshepsut's face paled; Meryet could see from the sudden stillness of the beads on her chest that the Pharaoh held her breath.

The pains again, Meryet thought. Hatshepsut often complained of sharp aches in her hip and thigh. Sometimes spells of weakness overtook her, too, and seemed related somehow to the mysterious, transient pain. Meryet wondered whether Hatshepsut's condition were not due to a lack of movement. Many months had passed since Senenmut's death. Hatshepsut's grief had stalled her. She was sedentary; she had grown stout with her own inactivity, though even subdued as she now was, she could not put off the air of regal command that was hers by nature. Even playing gently with Amunhotep, even stilled by her long sorrow, Hatshepsut spoke and moved with authority. When she spoke or moved at all.

"Do you suppose," Hatshepsut said, recovering herself, toying with Amunhotep's short side-lock, "you may have another?"

Meryet laughed. "One day, but gods make it not too soon. This one is enough of a handful for me, even with the royal nurses caring for him most of the time."

Batiret plied her fan on its long golden pole, swirling the flies away. "The Lady Horus would like an entire nest full of little Horuslings to pamper and spoil."

Hatshepsut grinned up at her fan-bearer with great affection, showing the charming gap between her teeth. "And why not? The world could use a few more of these." She tickled Amunhotep's foot; he squealed and clutched at his own soft belly in merriment. "The gods know there is precious little to be glad for in this life."

Meryet felt the smile slip from her face. No one wanted to rush Hatshepsut through her grief. Young though she was and relatively untouched by tragedy, Meryet still sensed intuitively that sorrow found its own route through the heart, wearing a crooked path, eroding the ka like a stream of water through dark soil until at last it sank away in its own time, and healing flowered in its place. But Hatshepsut's depression compounded Thutmose's guilt, and Meryet was left to impel him on his path. It seemed sometimes that she drove him against Hatshepsut's grief, goading him like a drover does his cattle. And Meryet was weary – Amun, but she was weary.

"Where is Thutmose?" Hatshepsut asked suddenly.

Meryet gave an involuntary jump, startled that the king had chanced so close to her private thoughts. "Drilling his soldiers. The southern circuit, I believe he told me."

"It's a good army," said Hatshepsut rather dully. "The new recruits seemed very sturdy."

Meryet doubted whether Hatshepsut had seen the new recruits. She nodded in agreement, careful to keep her skepticism well away from her face.

"Maybe we ought to find a sturdy soldier for this one, here." Hatshepsut jerked her head toward Batiret. "She should have a baby of her own."

Having finally convinced the troublesome flies to try their luck elsewhere, Batiret leaned casually on the shaft of her fan. "My steward Kynebu is sturdy enough for me. The last thing I need in my bed is a soldier, all muscle and no brains, stinking like horse piss."

Hatshepsut's eyelids fluttered in feigned shock. "What appalling language."

"And as for babies...." Batiret caught Meryet's eye, made a pinching motion with her fingers. Meryet covered her mouth with her hand. She had heard enough of the servants' gossip to know it was the sign they made at apothecaries' stalls in the marketplace, the silent request for the sticky acacia-gum suppositories that would stop a baby from growing.

"You have no idea how to behave yourself in the presence of royalty," Hatshepsut said, her mouth twisting wryly.

"The Good God would not have me any other way."

"It is good to laugh. You know, I haven't done it in ages."

"So I have noticed," Meryet said.

A clap sounded from the periphery of the garden, near the door that led into Hatshepsut's bed chamber.

"Come," the Pharaoh called.

One of her ladies approached, a young, inexperienced thing with the wide-set eyes and flat nose of the southern houses: the daughter of some minor noble working her family's way into the Pharaoh's good graces. The girl bowed awkwardly and held out a scroll. It was tied with a red thread, its knot sealed with a hard bead of wax. "A messenger arrived, Mighty Horus...Great Lady. He said this scroll was to be delivered into the hands of the Good God Menkheperre."

"The Good God Menkheperre is out drilling his soldiers," Hatshepsut said. There was a distinct note of annoyance in her voice. Meryet knew it must needle her, that Thutmose had become the one to whom stewards and ambassadors turned, to whom messages were delivered. And yet what else was Egypt to do? The country could not sink with her into grief. Life went on. Soldiers required drilling. Messages needed delivering.

Hatshepsut held out her hand. "Under the circumstances, I believe *Maatkare* may read the scroll. She is more than qualified."

Hatshepsut crushed the knob of wax between her fingers and waved the girl away. The scroll unrolled in her hands with a dry rustle. Her eyes passed over the contents, then narrowed. Her mouth pinched into an angry purse. She read the words again.

"Mistress?" Batiret said, her voice tense with worry.

"Kadesh." Hatshepsut spat the word.

"Ah," Meryet breathed. "I might have known. Another scroll about Kadesh."

"Another? How many have there been?"

Meryet and the fan-bearer shared a pained, helpless glance.

"Well?"

"Many," she finally admitted. "Thutmose has been working on..."

"Indeed! And I've been told nothing."

"As grieved as you've been, he thought it best to handle it himself."

Hatshepsut lapsed into a sulky silence. Amunhotep crawled to her lap, and she wrapped her arms around him. But her eyes remained distant and dark. "How long has this been going on?"

Meryet was uncertain whether Hatshepsut referred to the threat in Kadesh or her own disassociation. Either way, the answer was the same. "Months, Mighty Horus." She bowed in a semblance of apology, though the gods knew Meryet was not to blame.

"Then it is time something was done." Hatshepsut's voice snapped with command. Her eyes glimmered like dark points of fire on a high hill, alive with a keen glint that Meryet had missed for far too long.

CHAPTER EIGHT

THE SMALL ESTATE STOOD ON the bluffs above a long-dry ravine, an hour south of Waset by boat. A dusty footpath wended through a scrubby orchard of olives and apricots, rising sharply up the flank of a yellow bluff to the small but well-appointed home at its pinnacle. The roof of the estate was barely visible, peeking over the pale, new-quarried stone that had been used to increase the height of its outer wall. A guard moved along the line of the wall, tiny with distance, as black against the clear, bright blue of the mid-day sky as an ant against fresh-scrubbed tile.

Thutmose paused in the shade of the largest olive tree. It leaned across the footpath, exhausted by age. Only a few shriveled fruits clung to the tips of its gnarled branches. Most of this orchard was long past its fertile years; the estate was no longer producing, no longer particularly valuable to any noble house. Thutmose had procured it easily and quietly, working through a diffuse network of stewards and loyal nobles. It would be difficult for anyone to trace the property to the throne. Not that anyone was likely to come nosing around such a place. Still, a man could never be too cautious. He watched the guard on the estate's wall creep toward the southernmost corner, pause, turn east, and disappear from view.

"How many guards are on the house?"

The soldier Djedkare answered with his usual attentive

pluck. "Twenty, Horus. The barracks we built lies just beyond the house. You can't see it from here, but of course it is ready for your inspection, should you desire it. The men take it in shifts. There are never fewer than six men at watch on the walls or the gate, and twenty on site at all times. Occasionally more, when we receive supplies, or when the weekly shifts change."

Djedkare was not many years older than Thutmose, but already showed impressive aptitude. The man was bright, thoughtful, serious about his work. More importantly, he had spent his years of soldiering at foreign outposts, far from Waset and its royal family, yet his own family was known to be deeply loyal to Thutmose and Hatshepsut. The same was true of all the men who served here: strangers to Waset, but proven in loyalty.

They started toward the house on the bluff. Thutmose kept his eyes on his own sandals as he made his way up the lane, allowing Djedkare to lead the way. The man spoke all the while in his efficient, controlled clip.

"Lady Satiah has seemed entirely content, Lord. She has shown no interest at all in leaving. She is polite and pleasant whenever we have need to speak to her, and yet she is as modest as any man could wish. Keeps herself hidden from the eyes of men. Unless she has need of something her few servants can't fetch for her. We're so out of the way here, and the estate is so old that we have no unexpected visitors. No one comes poking about. I must say, it is the easiest guard duty I've ever done."

"I am glad to hear it – glad to hear you find the lady so agreeable."

Djedkare nodded. "If I am impertinent, I apologize humbly, Lord – but she seems the very best sort of woman, the kind even a king would be lucky to have."

Thutmose tried to stifle a laugh. It fought its way out as the merest exhalation, a soft snort of wry amusement.

"I hope I do not overstep, Mighty Horus."

"No, Djedkare; it's quite all right. Lady Satiah is the kind of treasure a man must guard very closely."

"Indeed."

The man would not press his comments further. Thutmose understood him well enough to know that much. Djedkare, like all the men who minded the estate, thought Satiah to be exactly what Thutmose had made her seem: a woman of interest to the Pharaoh, prized and respected, more than a concubine for the harem, but not yet officially a wife. He had allowed the men to speculate, as far as propriety would allow, that the Great Royal Wife struggled with the idea of Thutmose marrying another woman – not just adding another pretty and well-connected girl to his harem, but joining with another woman before the eyes of the gods, conferring upon her real status.

Thus, the guardsmen believed Lady Satiah was housed here, a pampered pet of the Pharaoh, until the gods saw fit to soften Meryet's heart.

None of these men would recognize Satiah for who she truly was. None would have had any significant chance to see her in her former life, when she had been Neferure the God's Wife, his original consort. They knew only what he told them, and believed the rumors they concocted over their nightly beer.

The gods keep it so.

The climb to the top of the bluff was hot and dusty. Thutmose ducked gratefully into the shade of the gateway and called for something to drink. Djedkare fetched a skin of wine; Thutmose drank deeply, not only to soothe his dry throat, but to still the anxious tremor in his hands. When he was ready, he told the men to open the gate.

One great cedar door, twice the height of a man, swung wide to admit him. Beyond the rebuilt wall, a small garden unfolded in the sun. It was newly planted, revived from the abandonment that had left the courtyard sere and unfriendly before Lady Satiah had moved in. But here, at least, she had done good and honest work. The flower beds were weeded, tilled, filled in with black soil from the orchard below – it must have been carted up by the guardsmen, one of the tasks Satiah had no doubt requested of them. A few pale green starts grew in the beds; some of them had been carefully staked and tied. Thutmose saw where cracked paving stones on the garden path had been repaired with plaster, and saw, too, the bright white of new plaster sealing the old dark tracks of leaks in the wall of a raised pond. It sparkled with water – that, too, must have been carted up the path by the guards, for this high atop the bluffs no well could reach deep enough to tap a reserve of ground water. Satiah had gone to great lengths to beautify her little prison. It was a humble and lonely place, but thanks to her touch, it was at least prettier than the tiny cell at the Temple of Min where Thutmose had found her.

He was about to send Djedkare ahead to announce him when Satiah herself appeared, framed in the deep rosy stone of a doorless archway. She was as tiny and light-boned as a bird, stark and dramatic in plain white linen against the violet of interior shadow. Thutmose halted on the garden path. She stared at him a moment, then went back inside without word or gesture.

"Wait for me here," he told Djedkare.

Thutmose blinked his eyes rapidly, striving to adjust his vision to the cool dimness of the house. The chill was refreshing. Small niches in the walls held statues of various gods, but nothing else adorned the walls – no tapestries, no murals. The perfume of sacred incense hung heavy in the air, undercut with the smoky char of burnt meat. A sudden gust from the orchard moaned in the windcatcher high above his head. Satiah perched silent and self-possessed on a rustic wicker couch, waiting for him to speak with her hands folded in her lap.

"You have made the garden quite lovely," he said awkwardly.

"It will be lovelier with time. Everything I planted is still new."

"May I sit?"

"This is your home, not mine."

Thutmose found a wooden stool against one wall. He positioned it across from her wicker couch, reluctant to come any nearer.

"I admit it is a prettier prison than the last one you kept me in," she said.

"I had no choice but to keep you there."

"So you think."

"How did you get out, anyhow?"

Satiah answered at once, in a voice so lacking in coyness or irony that he knew she believed it to be true, and knew he would get no clearer response. "The gods removed me."

"Yes, well. I wanted to be certain you are relatively comfortable here – you and the boy. Is there anything he needs?"

"His name is Amenemhat."

Thutmose said nothing. He held her black gaze steadily. When she looked away, it was with a light toss of her head, the beads in her braids chiming together like tiny sesheshet in a dark temple.

"Amenemhat," she said again, "and now that you have an heir, it is time you restored me to my position."

"Your position?"

"Great Royal Wife."

"Neferure," he said, but she hissed at him like a nurse quieting a difficult child. Thutmose bit his tongue. It would not do to allow the servants or the guards to hear that name. Inwardly, he cursed himself for a fool. *You cannot allow her to rile your anger.* "Satiah," he said calmly, "you know you are not my Great Royal Wife any longer. You never will be again."

He disliked the way she arched her brows at him, the cold consideration in her eyes, the stillness in her small, fine mouth.

"You won't be," he said, "not even if you should find some way to do to Meryet what you did to Senenmut."

"Meryet. Yes, I heard all about that one while working in the temples. Don't fear, Thutmose. I have no reason to do *that* to your precious Meryet. Hathor is satisfied with her drink of blood, and for all I know, she will remain so."

"For all you know?"

Satiah gazed at him placidly, her pretty, delicate face open and serene. "All I know is much more than all you know, Mighty Horus. Affairs of state are one thing; a king's duties at the temple are one thing. True communion with the gods – true *union* – is quite another." She leaned forward slightly. The reed wicker creaked, a sound that raised a chill on his arms and sent a sick thrill up his back. "I know you still see it in me, Thutmose."

"See what?"

"My power."

"Your power," he scoffed.

"You see me and you remember. The bull – my power."

"You never tamed the bull, *Satiah*. You were then and are still now nothing but a girl – a mortal girl."

"Speak those words all you please. You know you do not believe them. I am your wife – your Great Royal Wife. The gods made it so, and even a Pharaoh cannot undo it."

"I already undid it. I repudiate you."

She waved a hand, taking in the estate, the garden glowing in the bright sun through the archway, with one quick, bird-like gesture. "Then why all this? Why this lovely prison if you repudiate me, if I am nothing to you? Why so close to Waset? Why so close to your bed?"

"I keep you close so I can know where you are at all times. So there will be no knives stealing out of the shadows in my palace."

"Why don't you kill me?" She said it not in despair or hysteria, but in bland curiosity.

It struck him suddenly that although she may change her name and deny her heritage, she was still – would always be – the daughter of Hatshepsut. The daughter of the woman who took the throne, who led men in battle, who secured the treasures of Punt. She was the daughter of the one the soldiers called seshep – the daughter of the woman who pulled down a god. Satiah might dress in the plain linens of a priestess and toil placidly in her garden, but the calculation and cunning of a Pharaoh were hers by blood.

"Is it because of Amenemhat? Is that why you suffer me to live?" she said.

Thutmose rolled his eyes. "No. I cannot prove the boy isn't mine, and the circumstances of his birth are not his fault. I will not punish him – will even give him a proper upbringing in the palace, if that is your wish. But I will never look upon him as my son. It is not for his sake that I allow you to live. Don't think to use your son as your shield."

Thutmose rose from the stool. He tugged his kilt straight, felt the reassurance of the dagger concealed in the intricate pleats of his sash. Without another word, he turned for the doorway.

"I know," Satiah called after him. Her voice was musical, light, confident as a king's. "It's the Bull of Min you remember, Thutmose. You remember, and you fear."

He made his way through the garden without a word to the guards. They rushed to open the outer gate for him, and he was halfway through the orchard, Djedkare in silent tow, before he realized he had drawn the dagger from his sash. He cursed, thrust it back into the hidden sheath, but his fingers did not want to unclench from its cold, reassuring hilt.

CHAPTER NINE

HATSHEPSUT BENT OVER THE MAP. Her finger traced a line Thutmose had marked across the northwestern border with a stump of charcoal. She squinted; the brown of her bare lids showed through brilliant malachite eye paint in patches, evidence that she had rubbed carelessly at tired eyes. Thutmose gestured for a lamp. Hesyre fetched it at once, set it near the lady Pharaoh, and withdrew with a bow.

"I am not an ancient," Hatshepsut muttered without looking up. "I don't need to be surrounded by lamps just to find my way to the privy."

"It's my own eyes that feel the strain."

"Nonsense. You are hardly more than a child, Thutmose."

"I am a king as much as you," he said playfully.

The warmth he felt at the revival of Hatshepsut's ka was, he often thought, the only thing keeping him from descending entirely into madness. The strain of planning the campaign into Kadesh made him feel as addled as a toothless grandfather. At least he had the benefit now of Hatshepsut's assistance. It was a relief to pass some portion of the burden onto her strong shoulders. Knowing Egypt stood to lose that crucial corridor between the northern border and the fortress of Ugarit had roused her heart and ka from its long slumber.

"We must not lose Retjenu," she had declared, storming into his chamber one morning in her man's kilt, the Nemes crown flying back from her round face like the wings of a stooping falcon. "Treat with them, trick them, crush them – I don't care how it's done, but the trade routes must remain open, and indisputably ours."

They had begun that very day, closeting themselves in Thutmose's apartments with their maps and messengers' scrolls, with the reports of hired eyes they had both worked so hard to sprinkle unseen amidst the Retjenu populace. And they had kept at their labors, while the flood waters receded into the breast of the river, withdrawing once more into the vein of life that sustained the Two Lands – *their* lands, Thutmose's and Hatshepsut's. By the time the crops in the fields stood ankle-high, Hatshepsut was confident of their plan, her faith as solid as granite.

Thutmose still harbored doubts.

Now she looked up from the map, her finger absently pinning Kadesh to the papyrus. She spoke some words to him, but Thutmose never heard. The grayness of her complexion took him aback, and he stared at the darkness ringing her eyes, the weary set of her mouth, in dull surprise. It was not the first time her appearance had caught him off guard. Since Senenmut's death, the signs of some vague but undeniable illness had stolen over her features, and the illness seemed to make its mark more firmly known each day. She had grown plump with her own inactivity, and yet there was a haunting, alien frailty about her now, a quality which Thutmose could only call *gauntness* in spite of her extra flesh. The palace servants kept him well informed, and so he knew she suffered from fits of vomiting and weakness, though she never mentioned these spells to him or to Meryet.

He had called on the best physicians in Egypt, who examined her skin, her breath, her pulse, her morning urine. The best they could surmise was that her ka had suffered a great shock – an unsurprising revelation. They recommended poppy milk for plenty of restful sleep, and the smoke of semsemet to soothe the pain and stimulate the appetite. One physician had offered to cut into her scalp and remove a bit of her skull to release the demons that inhabited her body. The man barely left the king's apartments with his own skull intact.

Magicians, too, were ineffective. They prescribed particular songs and chants, amulets, beseechings to this god and that, and not a note or gesture of their efforts eased her discomfort. That chilled Thutmose. If even the gods could not lift this malady from Hatshepsut's body and kas, how long would she remain in the realm of the living?

At least this – the planning, defending Egypt – kept her tethered to the world.

"If the reports are correct," she said, bending over the map again, "there is a high pass here, above the town of Megiddo."

"A very narrow pass. Too narrow to move the army through at any useful pace."

"If you approach from any other direction, word will travel too fast. There will be too many shepherds in the lower hills, here and here. Sheep-boys can move quickly when they want to. Megiddo will be at the alert long before you arrive. They may even have time to call in help from their Hittite allies."

"I see the sense of it," Thutmose admitted. "But I don't like the idea of..." He cut off abruptly.

Hatshepsut's hands flew to her temples. She winced as she clutched frantically at her head.

Thutmose was around the table in a heartbeat, taking her by the shoulders, easing her back onto the silk couch. Her face had gone even paler, with a sickly hint of green about the mouth. He turned for Hesyre, but the man was already speeding forward with a large clay basin in his arms.

"It's all right," Hatshepsut said. Her voice quivered. "Only a spell of dizziness."

Hesyre set the bowl at her feet. "Go get Meryet," Thutmose whispered to his servant.

By the time Meryet arrived, flushed and wide-eyed, Hatshepsut was lying prone on the couch, one arm draped across her eyes to shut out even the meager light of the nearby lamp. She had heaved the contents of her stomach – not much more than thin yellow bile – into the basin, while Thutmose had watched helplessly. The spasms shook her body, wringing her out like an old, worn cloth. The sight of her gripped so completely by illness filled him with terror, and once more the guilt stole into his heart, coiled there like a waiting snake.

Meryet knelt beside the couch in spite of the nearness of the fouled basin. She took Hatshepsut's hand in her own. "We must get you back to your own chambers."

"No," Hatshepsut croaked. "Not like this. No one must see me like this. Only you and my own servants. The rest must not know."

"Nonsense," Meryet insisted. "Nehesi is just outside the door. If you are too weak to walk, he will carry you."

"She's right," Thutmose said. He laid a hand gently on Meryet's shoulder. "No one else must see her this way. The Pharaoh, carried through the palace like a helpless infant, for any ambassador to see? It would never do – especially now, with things in Kadesh as they are. Word might travel." He could feel Meryet's trembling, but she did not argue.

"Then I will stay until you are able to return to your chambers," the Great Royal Wife said. She pressed the back of Hatshepsut's hand against her cheek, and through the tremors of the illness, Hatshepsut managed a brittle smile.

Three days later, Thutmose summoned his wife to his chambers. Meryet looked nearly as drawn and pale as Hatshepsut had the last time he'd seen her, and for one terrible moment Thutmose feared the illness was spreading.

But the same haunted hollowness did not darken Meryet's eyes, and as he welcomed her with a long embrace and a kiss on her brow, directly below the rearing cobra of her golden circlet, he realized with a hot flood of relief that it was only exhaustion he saw on her face. *Exhaustion – nothing more.*

"How is she?"

Meryet shrugged. She turned her face away, but not before he caught the glimmer of tears in her eyes. "Not well. Her hip pains her terribly. The dizzy spells and weakness are upon her all the time, day or night. She has scarce been able to rise from her bed for three days. It was a wonder she walked back to her chambers on her own. The way she moved through the palace, so straight and calm, I thought the worst was behind her. But when we got back to her apartments, she just...crumpled. Like a bit of linen dropped to the floor. Nehesi caught her before she hit the tiles. No one saw – no one but her own servants."

"Just as she wished it."

"Yes. Gods, Thutmose. She can't go on much longer like this. She can hardly keep anything down."

"Semsemet?"

"It helps for a few hours, but it dulls her thoughts and she doesn't like the smell of the smoke, so she refuses it until the pain and nausea are so severe that she's nearly weeping."

Thutmose felt the knot of his guilt flex and hiss deep in his heart. It was Meryet who led him to one of his fine silk couches, and they folded themselves together, wrapped themselves around one another, clinging desperately to the comfort of strong, warm flesh. A great swath of time passed in silence while Thutmose stroked Meryet's back absently, breathing in the scent of her wig and skin: her perfume of roses and myrrh, a breath of dark wine, the faint, acrid note of the semsemet smoke from Hatshepsut's chamber. A white star crept across the bars of the windcatcher, which showed a pattern of deepest blue in the black darkness of the high ceiling. Thutmose was content to watch the star's progress, dozing a little, grateful to release his fearful thoughts into nothingness while he soothed himself with the simple pleasure of Meryet's skin.

At last, though, she broke the silence. "Thutmose, ought we to tell her?"

"About what?"

"About...the Lady Satiah."

Meryet knew, of course. There was nothing he kept from her – *almost* nothing. She had agreed with him, that it was imperative to keep Satiah close and under guard, to make her every movement known. The Great Royal Wife was not afraid, but she was cautious, and more so now than ever before. She had Amunhotep to protect, after all.

"It could give her some resolution," Meryet said. "If she is...if she goes to the Field of Reeds..."

Thutmose shook his head obstinately.

"*If.* If she departs, would it not be kinder for her to know that her daughter is alive and well?"

"I don't think so. Truly, I don't. I know her. She will never forgive what was done to Senenmut, no matter how long she lives, and the gods make it a long time yet." *She will never forgive what Neferure did, and I will never forgive what I did, forcing her to put Senenmut aside.* "No. She mustn't be told, Meryet. It would only pain her more."

I am sure of that, if nothing else.

CHAPTER TEN

THE SEASON OF THE EMERGENCE meant renewal, life, the comforting reassurance of an endless continuity. The dark silt of the Black Land erupted with green, a carpet of lush vitality that rippled in cool river breezes. The very land itself smelled wholesome, lively, young. It was a bittersweet counterpoint to the painful drudgery of Meryet's days. She had made herself the constant companion of Hatshepsut, who had not risen from her bed in weeks, except to relieve herself and bathe. This she did only with the help of her servants before sinking back onto her rumpled linens, clutching at her aching hip, her unpainted face ashen and beaded with sweat. While the Two Lands celebrated the god Waser's promise of endless renewal, Hatshepsut had fallen into a decline. The ecstatic singing of birds in the garden, overwhelmed at the abundance of new growth and insects to eat, seemed a cruel mockery of the Pharaoh's weak sighs and cries of pain.

The helplessness tore at Meryet – not only Hatshepsut's weakness, but her own lack of resources to offer. She could think of nothing more to do than to be present, to take Hatshepsut's hand when the pain overwhelmed her, to offer a strong arm to lean on when she hobbled to the privy. There was nothing a Great Royal Wife might do here, no command she could give that would chase the demons from Hatshepsut's body, no wise decision she could hand down that would make her husband see sense in the face of his grief and confusion. She could only sit on the stool beside

Hatshepsut's bed, unspeaking for hours, watching the sweat form and run on the Pharaoh's creased brow.

Occasionally Meryet would pace, crossing the length of the bed chamber six or seven times before wandering out into the garden. The sun there was too bright for her eyes, the flowers too flagrant, offensive with their bright colors and their cheery perfume. When she could, she would lose herself in stories, reading any escapist scroll her servants laid their hands on: implausible adventures in foreign lands, purporting to be true accounts; wild tales of the gods' dark wrath; light-hearted love stories in which the women sighed and the men killed lions with their bare hands to show what strong husbands they would make. The scrolls never kept her occupied for long. Sooner or later, her sense of duty would drive her back to Hatshepsut's side, and she would take up the cold hand and stroke it absently while pale-faced, stricken Batiret stirred the air with her fan.

On an evening two weeks into Hatshepsut's illness, Meryet returned from the garden and tossed her scroll onto the Pharaoh's little bedside table beside half a dish of cold broth and a few untouched pieces of bread. She was already beginning to forget the details of the inconsequential story. The garden had filled with the late hatch of mosquitoes, the familiar plague of cooler hours in the season's opening weeks. Hatshepsut's women were setting up braziers on tall tripods near the garden door, filling them with the pungent oil that drove the worst of the insects away. The women moved like dreams beneath water, rippling and slow in the twilight. Their lights cast a warm-colored glow into the bed chamber. A faint shadow of greasy smoke rippled along one wall, climbing up painted murals of Hatshepsut in better times, a young, strong king moving boldly across a brilliant and perfect world.

Hatshepsut lay with her eyes closed, either asleep or in too much pain for Meryet's usual attempt at lighthearted conversation. The Great Royal Wife was about to lower herself onto her stool to take up her vigil, but a clap came distantly through the great lifeless depth of the king's chambers.

Batiret's fan stopped moving; she turned dully toward the sound.

"Someone is at the door," Meryet said, surprised.

Batiret propped her fan against the wall, shook her arms to dispel cramps from hours spent listlessly waving the plumes. "I'll go and see." A moment later, the fan-bearer's head poked into Hatshepsut's bed chamber. "The Pharaoh, Great Lady."

It had been some days since Thutmose had come to Hatshepsut's bedside. There was no blame to offer in that. Someone must go on running Egypt while one half of the Pharaonic power lay stricken by the gods' inscrutable cruelty. Meryet would have helped him at his task, taken whatever she could of his burdens, but her ka kept her tethered to Hatshepsut's side.

She went out into the anteroom, suddenly aware that she was very hungry. Her stomach was hollow with grief and the length of the day; it ached to be filled, as her arms ached to wrap around Thutmose's body, to hold him close and feel the indisputable *aliveness* of his skin. She smiled to see that he had brought a basket of figs and fresh bread. They sat together on one of Hatshepsut's couches, sharing the food between them. The figs were so sweet she nearly choked. They weren't over-ripe, she knew; it was merely the sharp contrast they made to the bitterness of her days. The soaring ceilings of Hatshepsut's chamber seemed as far away as the night sky, still and dark in the weary silence of the chamber.

"How is she?" Thutmose asked.

"As ever." Meryet took his hand. "She is lingering; that's all. I can't stand to see her like this. Her pain is bad enough, but what truly tears at my heart is her weakness. She was so strong, Thutmose. There never was a stronger woman, not even in the gods' dreams. She led an army..."

"Built a great temple," Thutmose said, morose, his eyes far-off and dull, "brought the treasures of Punt to Egypt. She trampled a god. And now...."

Meryet embraced him, felt the words he could not bring himself to say quiver in his chest. "I know," she murmured.

She let Thutmose go reluctantly, handed him a piece of the bread. It was still warm from the ovens, its crust grainy with rich, coarse-ground bits of golden barley. Meryet tasted the bread herself. It was simple and good, a comfort so sweet it brought fresh tears to her eyes.

"I try to shelter her," Meryet said between bites, "from the news out of Kadesh. She doesn't need to think on warfare right now; she needs to...."

She needs to get well. The unspoken words hung heavy in the air between them.

At last Thutmose ventured, "If I don't leave Waset soon, it will be too late to stop Kadesh from taking Megiddo. If Megiddo is lost, the north may well be lost, too."

"Oh, Thutmose...all that your grandfather worked for!"

"I know."

"You can't let that happen, no matter what goes on here in Waset."

Thutmose turned to her with a great sorrow in his eyes, a shadow that cast itself heavily upon his stooped shoulders, his drawn face. He seemed on the verge of speaking, but his head jerked to stare over Meryet's shoulder. His black eyes widened. "Hatshepsut."

Meryet whirled, gathering up her gown to run back into the bedchamber, the blood roaring in her ears, fearful that she would find the woman gone. But she was not gone. Hatshepsut stood in the doorway to her bedroom, straighter than she had stood for weeks, leaning one shoulder almost casually against the gilded lintel. The exertion had flushed her cheeks a deep pink. The color made her seem almost healthy; a curious, potent vitality sparked in her eyes. It brought Meryet up short. She hesitated in front of Hatshepsut, then, as the Pharaoh let out a tiny gasp and sagged, Meryet leapt forward to catch her.

"I'm all right," Hatshepsut said.

Thutmose was there, too, fitting his strong shoulder beneath Hatshepsut's arm. "Mawat, what are you doing out of bed?"

"Set take you both," she growled, "I'm not an infant. Can't a woman walk about her own rooms?"

"You're too ill," Thutmose said. "Where are your women?"

"I sent them away."

Meryet led them to Hatshepsut's bed, turned back the linens and fussed with them. "Well, that was a foolish thing to do," she said brusquely, her hands busy with the useless work. "And more foolish of your women, that they actually left! Imagine."

"What do you expect them do when I give an order?" Hatshepsut said. "I *am* the king."

Thutmose helped her back onto the bed, propped cushions behind her shoulders. "I know, Mawat."

"I will always be the king."

He kissed her brow.

When Hatshepsut's women were retrieved from the garden shade and Thutmose had returned to his duties, Meryet resumed her vigil on the bedside stool. Hatshepsut stared levelly at her for a long moment, and Meryet, drained of words, could think of nothing to do but stare back. Finally the Pharaoh spoke. Her voice was quiet and thinned by the Set-damned weakness that plagued her, but steady and calm as only a king's voice could be.

"He will never leave Waset while I still live."

Meryet shook her head. No – she would *make* Thutmose leave, make him do his duty. She would find a way to convince him.

"He won't. He is haunted by guilt, Meryet. He will never leave my side while I draw breath, though the gods know what good it does either of us for him to stay."

"He will see sense. He *must*."

"Someday, child, you will understand guilt. You will know the weight of it, the way it hangs about your neck all the time, waking or sleeping. You will know how accustomed one becomes, in body and ka, to dragging it here and there. It becomes a part of your very self. You cannot set it down for a few hours, nor abandon it, nor cut it off and sail free like a boat loosed from its moorings. Guilt becomes duty, and duty becomes ka. And ka is life."

Hatshepsut sighed, let her head fall back on the silk cushions. She wore no wig in her illness, and her natural hair had grown long, a black thatch of tight curls shot here and there with strands of gleaming silver. Meryet wanted to reach out and pull the white hairs away, like plucking the fine lines of a spider's web from one's path in the garden.

"I could say I hope you will never know guilt, Meryet, but I am wiser than that by now. I think I've earned a little wisdom, for all my life's pains and follies. What has it all been for, if not to give me some small measure of wisdom? All men feel the weight sooner or later. All women, too."

"What is anyone to do about guilt?" Meryet asked it a little defiantly, her voice breaking, her throat constricting on the words.

"Why, *duty*, of course."

"You said duty is guilt."

"It is all one and the same – all of it."

"It is not. I refuse to believe you."

Hatshepsut turned to her with a wry smile. "It doesn't matter whether you believe it or not. You will *know* it one day."

Meryet felt a question rise into her throat. It tasted so

bitter, burning on her tongue. She swallowed hard, hoping to chase it away, but the question forced itself out from between her teeth.

"And now...now that you are..."

"Dying."

"Now, are you free from your duties, your guilt? Or does the weight drag at you still?"

Meryet feared the question would wound Hatshepsut, but the Pharaoh tilted her head in simple consideration. She gazed into the depths of her beautiful, quiet chamber, musing on the question. When she turned to Meryet again, her smile was sad and trembling.

"I had a love once. A woman – Iset."

"Thutmose's mother?"

"Yes." Hatshepsut paused. "She was my comfort, my companion, the sister of my heart. And yet I picked her up and wielded her like a tool, used her for my own ends, carved out my power with her. When she died, I thought all my kas would shatter from the grief. Worse than losing Iset was the knowledge of what I had done to her."

The king fell silent. She lifted the edge of her sheet, ran the linen absently between her fingers. Meryet waited.

"But I did not learn from Iset. The gods set her in my path, gave her to me, that I might learn. I paid no heed to the lesson. I used my own daughter the same way, and so the gods took Senenmut, and Neferure, too."

Meryet clenched her hands into painful fists; her nails dug into the soft flesh of her palms. *No – I mustn't tell her. Thutmose was right; I have to believe he was right. It would only wound her more, to know her daughter still lives.*

There was a rustle of soft linen outside the bedchamber door. A moment later, Batiret entered, her face downcast, her cheeks streaked with tears. She held a little cloth bag in her hands; her fingers were white from clutching the fabric in tight, trembling fists.

The woman's demeanor filled Meryet with sudden dread. "What is this?"

Hatshepsut sighed. "Maat. I have used others for my own ends all my life, Meryet. At least I might offer myself up now."

"Offer...?"

"For use. Gods, child – let me serve some purpose greater than my own power, greater than my pride, now that I stand at the end of this road. Let me undo some small part of the pain I have caused. Let me do it for Iset's sake, and for Senenmut's."

She held out a hand, beckoning to Batiret. The woman sank sobbing onto Hatshepsut's bed, stretched herself along her mistress's body, her face pressed into the linens. Hatshepsut stroked her fan-bearer's shoulder with a fond, gentle hand.

"What is in that bag?" Meryet jumped up from her stool. "Batiret, give it to me."

"She will not give it to you," Hatshepsut said quietly.

Meryet gaped at the king. A chill stole over her body, raising goose flesh on her skin. She shuddered. "You *can't*."

"Thutmose will not leave Waset until I am gone. You know it's true. You know there is nothing you can say to convince him to abandon me to my fate. He is crippled by his own guilt; his heart is in a fog; he cannot make the decision to go. Meryet, my dear daughter, you know you cannot sever the weight of his guilt from his ka. It keeps him tethered here, tied to me. It keeps all of Egypt tied to me, like a bird in a fowler's snare, while I linger. While I am useless. We must make this decision for him. We must free him to act. Let me be the knife that cuts the bird from the net. I will free Thutmose, that he might save Egypt from disgrace."

"There must be some other way – some way to convince him that he *must* go north. You still might recover your health."

"No," Hatshepsut breathed.

Meryet could see, in the starkness of her dark eyes, in their impossible depth, what it cost the king to say that single, small word.

Batiret raised herself slowly from the mattress, her pretty face flushed and distorted with sorrow. She opened the bag. Hatshepsut reached inside, withdrew a small clay vial sealed with a cap of yellow wax.

Gripped by desperation, frantic to cling to Hatshepsut as if she might hold her to life with her own arms, Meryet scrambled onto the bed. She met Batiret's swollen red eyes over Hatshepsut's body. Meryet did not know whether she ought to beg Batiret to stop this, stop Hatshepsut, talk sense into the Pharaoh – or whether she should permit it, throw up her hands and allow the gods to do with them all as they would.

Batiret reached out to clasp Meryet's hand. "She is right, Great Lady," the fan-bearer said in a trembling voice. "Only this will save Egypt. Let her free the Pharaoh to act."

Weakly, Meryet shook her head. She loved Hatshepsut too much to agree – to *permit* that she should die. "There is some other way; I know there is."

Hatshepsut gave a little laugh. It shook her diminished frame, and for a brief moment the fierce bravado of the king she had been shone once more in her face. The force of Hatshepsut's natural power subdued Meryet's fears. A slow ripple of calm spread outward from her heart.

Maat.

"You cannot stop me, Great Royal Wife," said Hatshepsut, her voice rich with humor, with determination, with love. "I am the king."

Meryet bowed her head in acceptance. *Amun, do with us all as thou wilt.*

She held out her hands for the vial, and when Hatshepsut

placed the cold clay in Meryet's palms, she worked the wax seal from its narrow mouth. It was Meryet who held the vial to the Pharaoh's mouth. A droplet of the poison beaded on Hatshepsut's lip. It was white as milk, thick like honey.

Poppy. She will feel no more pain, no more suffering.

Hatshepsut fell into a deep sleep, her chest moving steadily with her breathing, while Meryet and Batiret lay to either side of their king, wrapping her body with their young, strong limbs, washing her cheeks and forehead with their tears. Hatshepsut's sleep deepened, and deepened, going deeper than the river, deeper than maat, deeper than the black between the night's stars.

PART TWO

THE GOD ETERNAL

1461 B.C.E.

Chapter Eleven

ONE FINAL OBSTACLE LAY BETWEEN the armies of Egypt and the treachery of Hatti and Kadesh. The ridge of mountains rose above the valley floor, an unbroken line of high, jagged hills taller than any temple or obelisk, the peaks as fearsome as the teeth of a grinning lion. Thutmose stood with his back to the vast Egyptian encampment, staring up the steep flank of the nearest mountain. Ancient tracks of rivulets scored its dun-colored flesh, their crevasses sprouting with dense greenery. Bare rock lay exposed to the sun and wind like the old bones of some gigantic and long-dead beast. Thutmose felt the waning heat of the setting sun on his back, felt the last drying beads of sweat run down his shoulders and spine, painting streaks in the pale dust of long travel that covered his skin.

The sound of a man approaching came to him, but Thutmose did not look around. He could not tear his eyes from the mountains. Like a dead beast's spine – like a fallen, ancient thing, immovable, unchangeable.

"No matter how long you stare at it, Mighty Horus, you'll never make it crumble, nor bore a hole in it large enough to drive the chariots through." Tjaneni stood half a step behind Thutmose, hands on hips. "The only way beyond is two days to the south. The hills aren't so high there."

Thutmose made no reply. His heart scarcely registered Tjaneni's words. He had spent countless hours back in Waset

– weeks, months studying maps of the region. He had known the mountains existed, had known he must lead his army around them. Yet somehow he had not expected them to be so...*insulting*. These Set-cursed rocks were more arrogant than any king could ever hope to be. Pharaoh he might be – sepats may rise and fall at his whim, men may live or die, temples and gods prosper or perish – but Thutmose could do nothing to these mountains but stare.

The very fact of the mountains stirred the rage that had carried him this far, many days' march beyond the traditional border of Egypt – though *this* was Egypt, too, and had been since his grandfather conquered it. *It is my land*, his heart thundered, *and these are my mountains*. It seemed he should be able to strike them down with his fist, tear through them like a knife through wet linen.

The anger that had roiled inside him since Hatshepsut's death certainly felt potent enough to flatten a mountain range. It had blown his ships north like a gale. It had filled his horses with the speed and endurance of the gods. Now it broke in a desperate, furious foam against the bones of the steep hills, crashing like the salt waves beyond the Delta. His ka moved unceasingly like those very waves, pitching, tipping, roaring.

Tjaneni held out a skin. Thutmose took it absently and drank; the beer was flat and warm, but it tasted distinctly of home: Waset's fields dreaming peacefully of the harvest to come, the river moving slowly, grandly beneath the hot sky. All at once Thutmose missed Meryet and his son with a wrenching force. He nearly doubled over with the pain of his longing, and might have, had Tjaneni and the mountains not been there to see.

The scribe evidently saw the yearning flicker in Thutmose's face, for he said quietly, "They will be all right, Great Lord – your wife and child."

Thutmose nodded, and smacked the drinking skin into Tjaneni's chest with what he hoped was a confident smile. The man gathered up the skin with a look of concern writ plainly on his face. *Are my fears so easy for my men to see?* Thutmose asked himself.

He had done all any man or king could do to ensure Meryet's safety. He had assigned Nehesi to her service, admonished the man to be her shadow, day and night, now that his service to Hatshepsut was at an end. Nehesi was old, but still stronger than most men in the guard, and after so many years at Hatshepsut's side, he was wise in the ways of palace and court alike. And Nehesi had troops – enough trusted men that Meryet would only ever be out of their sight behind her closed chamber doors. Even then, they would patrol her rooftop, her garden wall, and would do the same for Amunhotep and his staff.

I must trust that it will be enough.

Satiah couldn't leave her own dwelling, much less work her way past Meryet's palisade of guards. Unless she truly had some magic, some divine intervention that spirited her beyond thick sandstone walls under the very eyes of alert palace watchmen. She had done it once. Might she do it again?

His fists clenched involuntarily at the thought. They rose of their own accord, and he was aware that he must look foolish, childish, on the verge of attacking the insolent mountains with knuckles and feet. But he could not make himself relax. It felt *good* to make a fist – good and right and maat, in a way that nothing felt maat anymore, for now all was a confusion of duty and guilt and rage.

"Lord," Tjaneni said, his voice mild and helpful, "may I suggest a visit to the priests' tent? You seem overtaxed by the day's journey. Perhaps quiet communion with the gods will aid you. I could arrange..."

Thutmose shook his head sharply, and Tjaneni fell silent, bowing his acquiescence.

The last thing Thutmose wanted now was communion with gods. Amun's eyes! It was the gods who maneuvered him to this trap, was it not? The gods who stirred his enemies to conspire, who allowed them to intrude on his grief over Hatshepsut. It was the gods whose wrath he feared when he forced Hatshepsut to put her lover aside – the gods who had made Thutmose their instrument in depriving her of happiness, before they callously snatched her off to the afterlife.

It was the gods who had seen fit to preserve Satiah in life while snuffing out Hatshepsut's flame all too soon. And Satiah – was he more furious with that demon of a woman, or with Amun and his kind? Thutmose could not decide. Satiah still had the power to manipulate him – still, years beyond boyhood, with the Horus Throne his, with all Egypt at his feet, with an army at his back. He was still the child tottering under the weight of the ceremonial crown, cowering in a field of emmer, watching that small, slender brown hand stroke the forehead of the great white bull.

His dread of the gods and of his sister weakened Thutmose. He hated himself for that weakness.

"Just tell my cooks to prepare a meal," he said at last. "And a bath of some sort."

Tjaneni turned at once to obey the command. When the man was gone, Thutmose told himself he would walk slowly back through the camp, seeing how his men and horses fared, making quiet preparations for the two-day trek south to the low mountain pass. He told himself he would do it, yet somehow he could not tear his eyes from the mocking face of the mountain. He still stood with his back uselessly turned to the camp when Tjaneni returned to announce that his bath was ready.

Inside the rough army tent that served as the royal accommodation, Thutmose stooped over a clay basin, wetting a scrap of linen to wash the dirt from his skin. No brazier was yet lit; the setting sun glowed through the heavy fabric of the walls. He closed his eyes and scrubbed at his face, listening to the musical sound of the water dribbling from the cloth back into the basin. The sound filled him with a curious poignancy, half rapture, half desperation. It was a singularly ordinary sound, simple and honest. Falling water always made the same soft music, whether it fell in the presence of a rekhet or a king.

When his supper arrived, a rabbit roasted whole on a fire-blackened spit and a few onions boiled in wine, he ate in silence, alone. The camp went about its nightly duties beyond his tent's walls, moving and rustling with quiet efficiency, fiercely focused on the days to come. Full dark descended on the valley. The red glow on the tent's walls was long gone. Thutmose left his tent, gave a few brief words of reassurance to his guards, and returned to the edge of the encampment.

The sight of that immovable wall of rock drew him, engrossed him with its might and the obvious futility of his cause. A flagrant banner of white stars waved behind the mountains' crest. The dark bones of the earth reared up, dense against the starlight, clenched like defiant fists. He thought maat might be enclosed in those stony palms, if only he could find a way to make them open and spill their truth, release the stifling grip on his heart.

The gods put these hills here, too, Thutmose mused. Another reason to scorn divinity.

Footsteps scraped on the faint trail behind him.

"Tjaneni."

"Ah, me again, Mighty Horus. I thought I might find you here."

"Are you coming to send me to bed, Mawat?"

The scribe chuckled. "It's my duty to record this expedition, as you commanded...."

"And your duty to shoot as many lying Hittites as you can with that remarkable bow of yours."

"It's the arm that draws the bow that's remarkable, Lord, not the bow itself."

In spite of his dark mood, Thutmose chuckled. "You are ever the modest one."

"Personal scribe to the Pharaoh – ought I to be modest?"

"Perhaps not."

"You forgot about the Retjenu."

"What?"

"I'll shoot as many of those toads as I will Hittites."

Thutmose thumped Tjaneni on his wiry shoulder.

"Easy, Lord, or you'll destroy the magic of the remarkable bow."

"Tell me, Tjaneni. Do my enemies know we are here?"

He shrugged. "If they don't know yet, they will soon. We can't move along the line of their mountain range for long without being sighted."

"It will take two days to make the southern pass."

Tjaneni nodded.

"And another day to cross it," Thutmose went on morosely, "and two more days to double back on Megiddo. Amun's eyes. We may as well blow on flutes and bang on drums the whole while, for all we'll take them by surprise."

The scribe sighed.

Thutmose turned back to his scrutiny of the dark peaks, as if some answer lay there. They looked different by starlight. The sharper, starker glow revealed new contours in the rock, filled the tracks of the ancient rivulets with shadow as black and precise as kohl around an eye. As Thutmose watched, some wisp of vapor moved across the sky, the breath of a cloud forming. Starlight and shadow rippled across the mountain's surface, and the deep black contour seemed to dip into itself, rolling and bending for the space of one heartbeat to reveal what Thutmose had not seen by the light of day.

A narrow cleft between two peaks, opening onto a flat,

stony path.

He recalled, with a pang of loss so sharp it threatened to make him cry out, Hatshepsut tracing a line of charcoal on a map, her eyes ringed in shadow. Thutmose lifted his chin, buoyed with sudden inspiration. *That's it.*

There, in that dark cleft, was the place where the jealous, hard-clenched fist of Amun would open. Thutmose would force it open, and cause maat to spill out across his land.

CHAPTER TWELVE

HATSHEPSUT RESTED FOR SEVENTY DAYS beneath the embalming salts. The season of Shemu dawned as Meryet and her son laid the Pharaoh to rest in the tomb of Thutmose the First. It had been Hatshepsut's wish to lie eternally beside the father she had loved so well as a child. The tomb's newly widened walls were painted afresh in preparation for Hatshepsut's funeral. The brightness of the colors seemed obscene, almost sacrilegious in the light of the priests' torches when they made their way deep into the darkness, bearing the nested and gilded coffins of the woman who had been king.

Meryet held Amunhotep on her hip in the orange light of the torches, spoke the words for him, guided his tiny hand to rest the sacred rod against the mouth of Hatshepsut's funeral mask. The boy looked with quiet solemnity into the lapis and ebony eyes of the mask, the precious stones set into a new skin of smooth, eternal gold. Amunhotep acted as the heir in place of his father, for Thutmose had taken the army north within days of Hatshepsut's death. The bird was freed from its snare.

Duty done, Meryet returned gratefully across the river and shut herself in her chambers, thinking to have an isolated cry with no one but Batiret for witness. The loyal woman had attached herself as fan-bearer to the Great Royal Wife's retinue, and Meryet was glad of her company. They had shared something of immeasurable import, that sad day when they had lain sobbing on Hatshepsut's bed, their fingers entwined and their tears mingling. Though she was only a minor daughter of an unimportant house, Batiret was as close now to Meryet's heart as any sister.

But a quiet moment with her new sister was not to be. When she arrived at her chamber door, Meryet found a young man waiting, bowing low over his clenched hands. He wore the red-striped kilt of a messenger. When he straightened, she saw that he clutched a small papyrus scroll.

Nehesi took it, broke the seal, read it with an ever darkening face. "You won't like this, Great Lady," he muttered.

Meryet ordered the messenger to wait outside while she swept Nehesi and Batiret into her apartments.

"A request for an audience," Nehesi growled when the door shut solidly behind him. "From the Lady Satiah."

Meryet lifted one brow beneath the fringe of her wig.

"Put her off, Great Lady," said Batiret. "She knows you will be off balance and fragile today. She only wants to prod at you until you topple. Don't give her the satisfaction."

"Batiret is right," Nehesi said. He crumpled the papyrus in his fist, then, with a guilty grimace, he smoothed it and handed it to Meryet.

She examined the note calmly. The characters were very fine and dainty, perfectly drawn without any flourish to waste ink. The wording was plain and respectful, not goading, but the timing was too deliberate. Meryet saw at once the good sense in Batiret's warning.

She was drained, body and ka, by the funeral ceremony, and yet more shaky and unsheltered with Thutmose so far away. But she *was* the most powerful woman in all Egypt now, and she would not shrink in the face of such an obvious and pitiful taunt.

"No. Let her come. If she wants an audience with the Great Royal Wife, then she shall have it."

"Great Lady..." Batiret began, but Meryet silenced her with a secretive smile.

"Send for a scribe, and fetch that messenger from the hallway, Nehesi. Tell the Lady Satiah that she shall have her audience this very afternoon."

When the double doors opened far at the end of the Great Hall, Meryet was already waiting on her glimmering seat. Behind her, the two empty Horus Thrones stood shining in a wash of lamplight, the flames dancing over every rich detail: every scarab, every god's face, every jeweled lion and leaping hare. She had instructed the hall's stewards to cast nuggets of myrrh into the lamps' flames so that the holy perfume of Punt drifted about her like an ethereal cloud. Behind the dais, figures of gods and kings stretched high along the wall, taller than three men, towering above the gilded thrones.

The faces of deities stared down from the caps of pillars flanking the massive length of the hall, their eyes upon the small figure in a simple white shift that made its slow, steady way across the slick sheen of the malachite floor. The ornateness of the hall itself served as a reminder to those who might think to challenge the House of Thutmose: the Pharaoh was chosen and sanctified by the gods. No one, not even a priestess, could undo their divine work.

Meryet watched with an emotionless face, gazing regally down from the height of her throne, as the tiny woman drew nearer. Satiah was indeed dressed as a priestess, as Meryet had suspected she would be. The unembroidered tunic of a temple servant, belted with the turquoise sash of Hathor, reflected in the deep green tiles like a wading bird's body in a still, tranquil pond. When Satiah came close enough that Meryet could clearly see the fineness and delicacy of her features, framed by the locks of a plain wig, her hands tightened reflexively on the arms of her throne. Had she been a seshep, her lion's claws would have dug into the throne until the gilding split. But her face remained composed, unconcerned.

In contrast to Satiah's frank simplicity, Meryet wore the full treasure of a Great Royal Wife. Her gown was the bright blue color of mourning, for this was still a funeral day, even if Satiah did wish to mock the occasion and toy with Meryet's grief. Meryet, for her part, would not disrespect the dead. The gown, however, hugged her hips and her narrow waist, revealing through its loose weave just enough of her navel and the crux of her thighs to ride the knife's edge of high courtly fashion. It was held by a red-beaded band that snugged tightly below her breasts, pushing them up and out, framing them between its gold-threaded straps. A broad collar of carnelian draped her shoulders and chest. Her wig was overlaid by flattened braids of gold, scaled like snakeskin so that each plait moved as she did, and fell down to her shoulders like a fountain of mid-day light. The alabaster wings of the Vulture Crown dropped to either side of her face, lending the sternness of the goddess Nekhbet to Meryet's countenance.

Nehesi waited at the foot of the dais, one hand on the hilt of his blade, restless as a pit dog. When Satiah was still several paces away, Nehesi held up his hand in abrupt warning, and obediently, reflexively, the woman stopped. She bowed fractionally, flashing her palms to the throne for barely a heartbeat. It was gesture of calculated insolence.

Meryet's mouth tightened. "Lady Satiah."

"Lady Meryet-Hatshepsut."

Nehesi took a menacing step toward the tiny woman. "You will address the Great Royal Wife properly, or I will personally see you returned to your *former quarters* in this palace."

"Forgive me, Great Lady," said Satiah, smooth and imperturbable.

"You asked for an audience, Satiah, and it is granted. Say what you will now, while I am still in a generous mood, for

I would sooner see you die than watch you draw another breath."

Satiah blinked. "Die?"

"A just payment for your sins."

"Ahhh," Satiah said, exhaling the word, raising her chin rather more than Meryet thought to tolerate. "It is the Pharaoh's place to decide who lives and who dies. It is not the work of the Great Royal Wife. Do you not agree? In any case, who indeed *is* the Great Royal Wife – you or I?"

"Mut preserve a fool," Meryet said with a light laugh. "What a dangerous thing to say."

"Dangerous? I think not, Great Lady. You are a usurper."

Before Meryet could answer, Satiah turned back toward the double doors and clapped. A woman entered hestiantly, carrying a large bundle in her arms. Nehesi shifted his weight as if he thought to draw his sword, but Meryet stayed him with a quick, subtle gesture. The woman at the far end of the hall bustled forward, and before she had passed the first pillar Meryet could see that she carried a child.

So Satiah has a baby. Did Thutmose know? He must be unaware. He told Meryet everything, but he had not told her this. Before the nurse reached Satiah's side, Meryet knew the child was a boy. What else could this ruse of an audience be about, unless Satiah intended to put forth a claim to the throne?

The child's face pinched; he was on the verge of fussing, but Satiah stroked his cheek tenderly and he quieted. Meryet sized him up in that moment, with Satiah's attention turned away from the dais, away from the startled expression Meryet struggled to ward away from her face. The boy was small, but he might just be the proper age to have been conceived while his mother was still Great Royal Wife. Or he might be too young by several months. She could not say definitively, and the uncertainty filled her with cold apprehension.

Thinking quickly, Meryet rose gracefully from her throne. "Walk with me in the garden, Lady Satiah."

"I prefer not..."

"You are under the mistaken impression that you have a choice in the matter. I am not interested in your preferences. You will walk."

Nehesi closed in, and Satiah, glancing at the blades weighing down the old guard's leather belt, nodded.

Meryet led her guest from the Great Hall, beyond the ambassadors' courtyard and into a wide, airy garden that ran down the length of the kitchens and storerooms. At the far end of the garden was the old wing of the palace where Satiah had once whiled away many long hours in isolation. When the woman saw the disued wing in the distance her mouth tightened; her eyes shone with a baleful fire, like cold, dark stars.

"Stay here with the child," Meryet told the nurse. The woman goggled helplessly at Satiah for a moment, but Meryet turned, knowing she would be obeyed – and indeed she was. She walked on with Satiah and Nehesi until they were well apart from the nurse and the boy. Meryet halted where several paths intersected, a place free of flower beds or shady stands of trees. They were well and truly alone here, and she could speak freely.

Satiah's boy had some features of the House of Thutmose – it was plain to see in his wide mouth, his strong nose and weak chin. But the same blood ran in Satiah's body as ran in the Pharaoh's, and mere resemblance was not enough to convince Meryet that this child was any threat. Still....

She rounded on Satiah. "You realize, *Lady Satiah*, that you must reveal your true identity if you think to claim the title of King's Mother. Thutmose was married to Neferure, not to *you*."

The tiny woman smiled placidly. "I must do no such thing. Neferure no longer lives. I am Satiah in truth. The power of the gods is with me; that is all the advantage I need."

"Who is the child's father?"

"Do you mean his earthly father, or his true father?"

"Do not try to frighten me. Your son was not sired by a god."

"Not *a* god...Great Lady." This last she added only after Nehesi's fist tightened on the hilt of his blade.

Meryet wrestled with a decidedly unregal scoff. "Which god, then?"

"All of them. I am their consort. I am their holiest vessel, and they mean the throne for my child." As she spoke, her eyelids grew heavy with remembered ecstasy. A tremor shook her small frame, as though an unseen power flexed and heaved inside her.

Meryet fought the urge to step away from Satiah. Instead, she forced herself to step closer. She could smell the old smoke of incense and charred meat on the woman's skin. Satiah gazed up into Meryet's face with complete self-assurance.

"So you think to threaten me with a child who *may* be Thutmose's son? Very well. If the boy truly is the Pharaoh's child, then he should be raised in the harem like a proper prince."

Meryet jerked her head toward Nehesi, and at once he called for a troop of his guards. They were always nearby, forever waiting on their leader's call like hounds eager for the hunt. The cries of the nurse tore across the emptiness of the garden as they pried the boy from her grip. The nurse set up a shrill wail, but neither Meryet nor Satiah looked glanced in her direction. Their eyes remained locked by the intensity of their mutual loathing, but Meryet saw something other than hatred writhe for one heartbeat in Satiah's wide-eyed stare: fear.

You wanted an audience with the Great Royal Wife, and you have had it.

Satiah recovered her composure, though not without visible effort. She painted a smile onto her lips. It was cold, but to Meryet's surprise it did not shake.

"You may return to your estate, Lady Satiah."

"Thank you." Satiah clapped her hands sharply, and the weeping nurse quieted herself. "Take good care of the heir until it is time for him to claim his throne from you and your husband, *Great Royal Wife*. I charge you with his well-being. The time is coming soon when he will rise up to take back what is his. I have no doubt of it. The gods will not suffer this farce much longer – of that I can assure you."

"Go," Meryet said, shutting her ears to the crying of Satiah's son as the guards carried him off toward the harem. A weight of loathing settled into Meryet's gut. "Before I cut your throat myself, Lady Satiah. Go."

CHAPTER THIRTEEN

THUTMOSE WAS AWAKE WELL BEFORE he heard his guard exchange a few low words with the scouting party. He and Tjaneni had retired to their tents to catch a few hours' sleep before the morning's march, but Thutmose had drifted uselessly in and out of slumber on his traveling cot, plagued by slow, transient dreams of Meryet rising from her bath, and of Hatshepsut leaning against a golden door frame, staring at him with demanding eyes that sparkles like winter stars in her drawn, sagging face. When he was certain the voices he heard were those of his scouts, he rose from his bed, grateful to leave behind the restless realm of sleep.

Outside his tent, the sky was a cold gray. Dawn was still distant by an hour or more. The Egyptian encampment spread for spans along the base of the mountain ridge, hundreds upon hundreds of tents standing pale and severe against the darkness of the night plain. He had twenty thousand men all told, eight thousand chariots...and yet it may not be enough to win back the passage to Ugarit, for there were days yet to lose in the march.

Amun damn me, I should have left Waset weeks sooner. But I could not leave her...not while she still lived.

The scouts bowed low as Thutmose's tent door swung closed with a soft thump. Tjaneni was there with them, watching Thutmose's face with a steady intensity.

"Mighty Horus," one of the scouts whispered, "we have

done as you commanded."

"Good. Tjaneni, wake my staff; have them feed these men and bring them beer. Then fetch all my generals. I would hear what my scouts have to say this very hour, before the sun rises."

The generals were not long in coming, though even in the pre-dawn gloom Thutmose could clearly see the traces of their interrupted sleep, the squinting eyes, the red tracks pressed into the flesh of their faces, evidence of rough packs used in place of proper head-rests. They gathered in a loose circle around the door of his tent while the scouts, fed and well recovered from their adventure, told what they had seen.

Above the encampment, in a place concealed by an outcropping of rock, the ridge was cleft by a high pass. It was a steep climb on this side, they told him, but beyond the grade was somewhat gentler, dropping down onto the fields surrounding the city of Megiddo. The pass itself was treacherously narrow, wide enough for the chariots to move in single file. There were no signs of recent Retjenu activity in the pass itself; it was apparently considered too narrow or too hidden to bother defending.

When the scouts had related the tale, Thutmose turned expectantly to his generals.

"It doesn't sound promising," said Pihuri. "The climb is steep – we risk the horses' legs."

Sikhepri agreed. "And one chariot at a time? Should the Retjenu suddenly decide the pass is worth defending after all, we would be like ants on a stone, and they would crush us as easily as a boy stamps his foot."

Thutmose looked at Minhotep, the most level-headed and careful of all his generals. "I think," Minhotep said slowly, "the passage to the south is much safer. True, we lose some element of surprise by going south – or even north, where the more remote pass lies – but the going will be easier, the men and horses fresher, your resources intact and fully accessible for the duration of the march."

"Indeed, the southern route sounds like the more sensible approach," Thutmose said.

His generals nodded in unison.

"And that is why we will take this pass."

Pihuri, startled out of all propriety, sputtered. "What? Great Lord..."

Thutmose raised a hand to forestall their protests. "Wake the army. I want the first ranks ready to follow me up the mountainside within two hours, fully armed and prepared for hard battle."

His generals staggered into the night to carry out his orders, and Tjeneni slipped to his side as quiet and unobtrusive as a shadow.

"Lord Horus," Tjaneni said, "please allow me to speak plainly, for your sake."

"All right. Speak away."

"Is this the wisest choice? Do you give this command because it is a superior strategy, or do you give it because your grief makes you reckless? I would ask the king to think on this question, and to answer it honestly in his heart."

Thutmose found his scribe's shoulder with his hand. He gave a rough squeeze. "I have asked myself that question already, Tjaneni, a dozen times."

"And what is the answer?"

"You don't believe it's a good strategy?"

"Strategizing is not my strength – only firing my bow."

"Do you trust your Pharaoh, Tjaneni?"

"Of course, Lord."

Thutmose thumped him on the back. "Good. That's all I need from you – from you or any of my men."

He strode ahead, returning to his scrutiny of the black wall of rock, leaving Tjaneni to see to the preparation of the royal chariot. He hoped his scribe did not notice that Thutmose had given no answer to the question. Thutmose had asked himself already whether it was strategy or rage that drove him, but had yet to find the answer within his own heart. Even now, with his army stirring to life at his back, he could not predict what the coming morning would hold.

The sun was no more than a hand's breadth above the horizon when Thutmose's chariot left the steep, rocky slope behind and gained the level ground of the pass. Two upthrust stone walls stood close to either side, towering above him as the driver reined in. The pass was indeed narrow, as the scouts had warned. Thutmose could have reached out an arm and brushed the rock wall with his fingertips, had he wanted to drop his spear. The passage was perhaps two dozen strides in length. At its far edge, the path dropped out of sight to the valley beyond. He could see fields and villages on the plain below, their colors just beginning to warm in the glow of morning. No warning shout was raised from the opposite slope, no cry of alarm. The only sounds were the trilling of birds and the singing of morning insects. The pass was, as the scouts had asserted, abandoned.

"Drive on," Thutmose said.

The chariot picked up speed. Soon the rock walls fell abruptly away, and the full force of the morning sun struck Thutmose, heating his great, heavy suit of overlapping bronze scales, beating against the hardened blue leather of the king's war helmet. From behind he heard the rapid rumbling of more chariots moving swiftly through the pass, the snorting of horses, the tight, gruff commands of his generals and the answering barks of his men. One at a time, they filed between the walls, fanning onto the slope below, arranging themselves into a great curved wing-like formation with Thutmose at its forward tip.

A man in a dust-colored robe rose suddenly from the rocks of the slope, staggering, evidently roused out of careless sleep. Thutmose raised his spear, but before he could thrust, the man fell backward with a gurgle, the goose fletching of an Egyptian arrow sprouting from this throat. Thutmose glanced over his shoulder in time to see Tjaneni drop his right arm to his quiver, nock another arrow with calm assurance as his chariot took its position beside Thutmose's.

A handful of Retjenu guards rose up like weeds from among their rocky hiding places, and were felled just as quickly by the bowmen. One or two managed to scramble out of bowshot, pelting down the hill toward the city of Megiddo.

The city crouched behind its walls at the pinnacle of a small hill, encircled by the pale band of an ancient, hard-packed road. Far beyond Megiddo's walls, at the northern and southern extremes of the valley, Thutmose detected wide blurs of smoke and dust, the distinctive haze that hung over army encampments.

"They've divided their forces," Thutmose shouted to Tjaneni and Minhotep in their neighboring chariots. "They knew we would take either the southern or northern routes, so they left the city unguarded to intercept us."

"Not entirely unguarded," Minhotep corrected. "Look."

One or two of the Retjenu scouts had reached the valley floor far below. As Thutmose watched, the tiny form of a runner sped along the pale line of the road, kicking up a weak banner of dust. A small stone building, a way-house of some sort, squatted in the roadside brush. No doubt a guard waited there with a warning horn to alert the city to the attack. But with the majority of the Kadeshi and Hittite armies obviously split and waiting at the distant ends of the valley, there would be little the city could do to halt Thutmose's advance.

His wing was assembled now, a great arc of horses champing

eagerly at their bits, of men lifting their spears to jeer down at the city and its absent army. Two more wings would yet form as the remainder of his army came bursting through the narrow pass. They would sweep down the mountainside in succession, catching up any straggling Retjenu forces like fish in a net. Thutmose gave the command, and with a cry that shook the very bones of the mountain, the Egyptian army took to its fierce, violent flight.

A frantic horn blared, the sound hardly rising over the roar of wheels and hooves. It was thin and distant; the weakness of the sound sparked a predatory fire in Thutmose's belly. As they thundered down the mountainside, he could see Megiddo stir to frantic defense below him. Men appeared along the walls, perhaps as many as two thousand. Like a rude gesture, the purple flag of Niqmod, king of Kadesh, lifted into the morning air.

Thutmose raised his spear in answer.

CHAPTER FOURTEEN

"IT WAS THE MOST DIFFICULT thing I ever had to do, you know," Meryet said.

She rested in the shade of her great sycamore, the broad, spicy-smelling leaves rustling overhead in a lazy breeze, while Batiret stood with hand on hip, watching the boys chase each other down the garden path. Amunhotep and Amenemhat toddled from shade to light, giggling and squealing, their little side-locks bouncing as they ran.

"Tearing a child away from his nurse and mother – imagine. And yet what else could I do?"

The boys' nurses – a new one for Amenemhat, approved by the Great Royal Wife – went scuttling after them. They rounded a bend in the path. A bank of blooming roses shielded them from sight, but the laughter of the little boys filled the garden with sweet song.

Batiret returned to the bench and took up her stitching. She was quite accomplished with a needle, when she wasn't chasing gnats away with her fan, and she had set about embroidering all of Meryet's older gowns with the intricate hem patterns that were growing in popularity among ladies of the court.

"You could have done nothing else," Batiret assured her, not for the first time.

Meryet patted her knee in gratitude. Sometimes this was

121

all she needed: confirmation that she had moved wisely – as wisely as anyone could, caught off guard as she was by Satiah's sudden appearance with her child.

"What was she thinking, after all, bringing the boy here? Did she assume I would bow down to her and hand over the throne?"

Batiret smiled. Meryet was glad of her friend's patient ear. It was the same conversation they'd had dozens of times already, the same thoughts, half angry, half sorrowful, that Meryet had voiced again and again. She had trodden this ground endlessly since Thutmose's departure for the north, months before.

Amenemhat was the kindest, gentlest child she had ever seen, small for his age – or his *supposed* age, at least – but bright and obedient. His nurse reported that he often asked for his mother, but seemed content enough with the nurse's rote reply that his mawat was away, and he must stay here with his aunties until she returned. The boy never cried or fussed over his situation, from all Meryet heard. She was grateful for that small mercy. If Amenemhat suffered in his captivity, or in his separation from Satiah, she could never have faced her own reflection in the mirror.

Meryet sighed. "I still feel terrible over the whole mess," she murmured, though Batiret had said nothing. "Perhaps I always will. He's such a sweet boy; it's a shame for him to be caught up in a political tangle. It's not his fault his mother is a viper."

"True," Batiret said, bending over her needle and bright threads. "And yet she *is* a viper. You know, Great Lady, that you can never return Amenemhat to Satiah's care."

"I know," Meryet said miserably.

"She will only try to use him again, to gain some leverage over the throne."

Meryet nodded. "At least Amunhotep loves him well. They are as close as brothers. I can be glad the boy doesn't suffer here. He is as happy as a child can be, playing with the King's Son."

Batiret let her needlework rest in her lap. "How long can we expect that to last, I wonder?"

"I don't know," Meryet admitted. "Many years, I hope, but no one can say. Amenemhat is a bright boy. Eventually he will wonder what place he has in the court. He will ask questions."

Batiret, silent and very still, leveled a dark gaze at her mistress.

"I won't do away with him," Meryet said. "Whatever you are thinking. I can't poison a child."

"Not all poisons are unkind." Batiret's voice was very low. "You and I know the truth of that."

"Still. I won't have it done, by my hand or any other, Batiret."

"As you say, Great Lady."

Meryet gazed off into the depths of the garden. It seemed absurd, to feel so morose on such a fine day. The flowers bloomed in profusion, filling the warm air with their intoxicating perfumes. A pair of flame-orange butterflies tumbled languidly across the path, their wings flashing in the sun. One of her maids laughed as she chased after a tame gazelle fawn – the little thing bounded on its spindle legs, leaping through the flower beds, the very embodiment of carefree joy. A copper bell tied around its tawny neck chimed gaily. In the distance, from the vicinity of the garden lake, she could hear the little boys laughing as they splashed in the water with their nurses.

"Do you know what troubles me so about Amenemhat, Batiret?"

The fan-bearer waited in silence, and Meryet ordered her thoughts carefully before she spoke on.

"It's the fact that he might, after all, have some claim to

the throne."

"Great Lady?"

"He may be Thutmose's child, conceived while Satiah was...was still Great Royal Wife."

Batiret's mouth thinned in a show of skepticism. "I think he is too young. I think the lady conceived him with some rekhet street trash, well after she was put aside."

"He resembles Thutmose so closely."

"His mother shares your husband's blood. The resemblance means nothing."

"Even so, the resemblance might be enough to convince powerful houses, if she ever chose to press the matter."

Batiret grunted. "Why not kill the viper and have done with it? She will plague your house until somebody does away with her. She's worse than a nest of rats in the cellar."

"I know." Meryet rubbed at an ache forming between her brows. "I know; I've told Thutmose the same thing. I've all but begged him to see to it, but whenever I bring it up, something akin to...to *fear* comes into his eyes."

"Fear? What does a king have to fear from a tiny thing like Satiah?"

"I wish I knew."

A sobriety came over Batiret's face, stilling her pretty features. "In spite of my own doubts, Great Lady, you are right. Amenemhat *could* be used as a tool again, to chip away at the throne."

"We must keep him close and under our influence until Thutmose returns from Megiddo. If the boy's fate is to be a tool, at least let us keep that tool in our own hands."

"The Pharaoh has been away for nearly five months now. It seems such a long while."

The ache in Meryet's head grew more persistent. "It does. His most recent letter said the siege of Megiddo is going well.

The Kadeshi forces returned shortly after he laid the seige, but the city is on a hill, and once our men were atop the hill, they were well able to crush the Kadeshi army's attacks from the plain below. Most of the Kadeshi soldiers were killed, and the remainder fled into the mountains. Now it's only a matter of cracking the city's walls, but they can't hold out much longer."

She hoped it was true. Her fears over Satiah's motives grew more pressing by the day, and Meryet found it increasingly difficult to maintain attention to her daily audiences. If only Thutmose would return! The burden wouldn't be so difficult to bear with him by her side.

Of course, with Thutmose returned, it would be plain enough for all to see the resemblance he bore to Lady Satiah's boy.

"It strikes me," Meryet said slowly, testing the words on her tongue, "that if Amenemhat's link to royal blood is severed, it won't matter who he looks like, or what any noble or priest sees in him. It won't matter who tries to wield him as a tool against the throne."

"Severed, Great Lady? But Lady Satiah..."

"*Says* she is only Lady Satiah, I know. But you of all people know how far she can be trusted, Batiret. You have the scars to prove it."

Batiret rubbed absently at the pale lines marring her upper arm.

"If she ever decides to reveal her true identity, Amunhotep's claim as heir would be threatened."

"Then what must we do to protect your child?"

"We must find some way of disinheriting Satiah's boy – of disinheriting Neferure herself."

"But how?" Batiret shook her head. "Gods bless us, Great Lady, the names of Neferure and all her royal family are carved into the very stone of Egypt. How can we undo that?"

"I don't know yet," Meryet admitted.

Amunhotep's nurse approached, carrying the sleepy child in warm arms. The boy was nodding, struggling to stay awake, to continue his play. Meryet stood, held out her arms to take the boy. He murmured against her neck. The weight of his body was dear in her arms, a wealth too precious to ever let go.

"I don't know yet how it will be done, Batiret. But I will find a way."

CHAPTER FIFTEEN

EGYPT WELCOMED ITS KING HOME to Waset with celebration and ceremony in equal portions. The priesthood of Amun waited on the quay when Thutmose's great blue-hulled war ship tied on its lines. They set up a chant of praise to the god as soon he appeared on deck, thanking Amun for extending his hand of protection over the king. A cloud of incense drifted across the clean-swept stone of the landing. The High Priest in his leopard-skin mantle raised an ankh on a gilded pole, praying fervently for the health of the Pharaoh, but Thutmose could not discern more than a handful of words over the chorus.

A massive, ornate litter, open to the sky, waited to carry him to the palace. When he had received the blessings of oil and salt from the High Priest, Thutmose sank onto the litter's throne with a sigh of relief. Hard as the seat was, it was infinitely more comfortable than his traveling cot and the tent he had called home during the long months of the siege. The familiarity of Waset was a balm to his troubled ka – its houses leaning close together like women gossiping at a well, its sounds of laughter and work and Egyptian voices, the sharp, rank odors of fish and still water, of refuse and industry.

More welcome still was the sight of the palace walls shouldering above Waset's rooftops. In the sunlight they seemed almost golden, glowing with warmth just for him. Though he lifted a hand now and then to acknowledge the shouts of his people, the bundles of flowers strewn in the path of his litter-bearers, he rarely took his eyes from the palace. As it rose slowly before him, it seemed to throw arms of comfort wide, pulling him into its embrace. This was home. This was where he belonged. And inside....

When his litter sank to the ground, Thutmose had to sit still for a moment, gripping the arms of his throne, stifling his urge to spring across the courtyard like a frantic gazelle and sweep Meryet into his arms. She waited like a vision, glowing in the eye of Re, a halo of sparkling dust motes limning her slender body. Her fine gown was a celebratory yellow, her jewels all turquoise and deep, lustrous malachite. But none of her finery was half as lovely as her face, open and serene, fine-made and glad – glad to see *him*. When he was certain he could rise and walk to her like a dignified king, and not run to her like a wild boy, he stood. The feel of her soft body in his arms, the sweet smell of her skin beneath spicy perfume, set a tremor running through his limbs.

"Gods," he whispered into the braids of her wig. "I have missed you."

She drew away from him, tears sparkling in her eyes like the motes that floated around her shoulders. At her gesture the nurse brought Amunhotep forward, and the breath caught in Thutmose's throat. The boy had grown so much in seven months. How was it possible? He tasted bitter regret at the back of his throat, that he had missed any part of his son's life. But he had saved the northern trade route, re-established Egyptian dominance in Retjenu, crushed the treachery of Hatti. All for this boy – for Amunhotep's inheritance. *The whole world will be yours*, he promised Amunhotep silently as he took the child in his arms.

Meryet threaded her arm through his and led him to his chambers, as casually as if he had never left.

I'm home, said Thutmose's heart with every grateful beat. *Home*.

Later, when they had bathed and called the servants in with clean bed linens, and then tangled the linens a second time, Thutmose lay propped on one elbow, tracing the shape of Meryet's body with a long, silky lotus petal. He had plucked the lotus flower from her wig as he undressed her, and now it lay bruised and trampled somewhere on the floor below. The single, sweet petal was all that was left of it. He tickled her throat with it, and she batted playfully at his hand.

"I'll never leave you again," he vowed.

"You will. Pharaohs always leave." She affected a pout. She was not very convincing; the woman was too sensible to pout over duties of the throne.

"Then I won't leave again too soon."

"Now that is a promise I can believe."

"There will be a feast tonight," Thutmose said. He was eager for it. Army rations were dull and uninspiring, and it had been a very long time since he had watched women dance, or delighted to the thrills of acrobats and magicians.

"An absolutely huge feast. I've arranged it all. Everyone will get so drunk, none of the nobles will be able to find their way out of the Great Hall, and they will all crawl under the tables to sleep like fattened dogs."

Thutmose laughed. "Good. I intend to get drunk myself."

Meryet rolled against him. "Don't get too drunk. It's been a long seven months for me; I'll be expecting more of this after the feast."

"Gods! At this rate, I'll have another son before I know it."

Her expression grew suddenly serious.

"What is it, Meryet?" He tried to tickle her with the lotus

petal again, but she moved his hand away firmly. There was nothing playful in the gesture now.

"Thutmose, I know about Amenemhat."

His face fell. He could think of nothing intelligent to say, so he stammered out, "I see."

"Not long after you left – in fact, the day...the day we buried Hatshepsut – Lady Satiah requested an audience with me."

"You refused, of course."

"No, I did not." Meryet's chin lifted in defiance. "She thought to see me weakened before her, with my husband gone and the strain of a royal funeral fresh in my heart. Instead, she saw me strong as a lioness."

"There is no other way anyone can see you, Meryet."

"There is." Her voice dropped to a whisper, lanced by a peculiar pain.

Thutmose stroked her shoulder, hoping to give her some small comfort with his touch.

"She brought her son with her. It is plain to see the resemblance he bears you."

"He may not be mine. The boy is small – I've seen him. It's difficult to determine his exact age, and Nefer...*Satiah* won't tell. In any case, she *is* my half-sister. That could be where the resemblance comes from."

"I know. I considered that, too. Still, she brought the boy to me in an attempt to frighten me. She thought she could intimidate me, put me off balance. Perhaps she thought she could move against me right then, with you away...send me off in disgrace, claim her rights as the mother of the heir, and be waiting in my place to greet you when you returned from Megiddo."

Thutmose could not suppress a shudder at the thought.

"I didn't let her win," Meryet said. To Thutmose's surprise, a note of self-loathing crept into her voice. Her eyes clouded. "I took the boy from her."

"You took him?"

"Yes. He has been with us the whole time, living in the harem. Oh, I've given him a fine nurse and guards to ensure he stays put. He has a little room in the House of Women, as is proper for a king's son. He *may* be your son, after all; we can't know for sure. He plays with Amunhotep. They're good friends – they're as close as brothers." She raised a trembling hand to her face to hide her eyes, as if in shame. "I can't forgive myself for it. Taking a child from a mother – even from a beast like Satiah – it's unthinkable, Thutmose. I am a mother myself. And the poor boy – he's a good lad, all the women of the harem say so, but he asks for his mother every day. Oh, the gods will curse me for it."

"No," Thutmose said gently. "They will not. You did the right thing – the best thing you could do, given the circumstances."

"Thutmose, I can't help but wonder what will become of the boy."

"Why, we'll raise him in the harem, of course. He will have a fine place at court, be a loyal servant to Amunhotep one day."

"I hope so. It's what I would like – the best outcome we can pray for, in a rather miserable situation. But Thutmose, you know Satiah intends to use him, and you know what she will do."

Thutmose nodded. He stared at the bright mural on his chamber wall, seeing nothing of the celebrated exploits of past kings. He saw only Neferure's face staring back at him, her eyes cold and calculating. "She will reveal her identity," he said slowly, musing, "and try to claim the throne for Amenemhat."

Meryet found his hand beneath the linens. The lotus petal crumpled between their fingers. "There is a way to stop her."

Thutmose looked at her dumbly. He knew the words she would speak, but his heart quailed even before he heard them.

"I have thought about it often," she went on, "the whole time you've been away. You must disinherit Amenemhat. Absolutely and irrefutably."

"But he is not even my heir."

"It is not *his* claim you must fear. Neferure was Hatshepsut's heir. If she lives, then she is the heir still."

"She never wanted the throne for herself," Thutmose said slowly, piecing the pot shards together at last. "But she does want it for her son."

"She can pass it to him. But only if she is still the heir."

Thutmose gathered his wife tightly against his chest. "Gods, but I thought I left the battles behind me in Megiddo."

Meryet sighed. "I'm afraid, my love, that a great war has only yet begun."

Chapter Sixteen

STARLIGHT BRIGHTER THAN ELECTRUM FLOODED through the pillared wall of Meryet's bed chamber. The night was young and fresh, the air heavy and rich with the promising fragrance of water to come. She pulled a heavy robe close about her shoulders and made her way out into the garden. A tinge of blue still clung to the sky, the deep, dark blue of wet lapis stone. She saw a brilliant white fire amid the black branches of her tall old sycamore, that dear friend who had provided her shade and a refuge from the pressures of duty more times than she could count. A breeze stirred the tree, clearing her view of the sky for one heartbeat. There it was: the full, glimmering orb of the star Sopdet. A new year had come.

Two sets of light footsteps sounded on the path behind her. Meryet did not need to look around to know that her twin shadows had followed her here, as they did everywhere. Batiret, slender and pretty and thoughtful in her duties, and Nehesi. The guardsman was advanced in age now. His untrimmed hair often peeked from beneath his wig, grizzled and thin. The lines of his face were deep now, but rather than giving him the softness of old age, they only made him sterner, more imposing. He was still as strong as a bull, and always would be, for all Meryet could tell.

Both servants had passed to her from Hatshepsut's keeping. In their comfortable presence Meryet still could feel the departed Pharaoh's many kas watching and, she hoped, approving.

"I'm all right," she called to them softly, automatically.

They were beside her now, following her gaze up into the sky. The stars were so numerous they seemed to shout a glad, clamoring chant among the branches of the sycamore. But Sopdet was brightest, and it burned like a temple fire.

"A new year," Batiret said. "Festival time. Nehesi will drink too much again and ask me to marry him."

Nehesi coughed to clear his throat.

"You had better not accept," Meryet teased. "He asks all the pretty girls to marry him when he's drunk."

"Well do I know it."

"If a man never asks," Nehesi said good-naturedly, "he can never expect to receive."

Batiret sniffed. "Women might prefer to be asked by a *sober* man. And anyway, you know I have a husband."

"That scribe you never see? Bah! He has arms like twigs. I've got much more to hold onto. Here..." Nehesi flexed his arm to show Batiret his muscles, "and here..." he made as if to grab for whatever he had beneath his kilt, but Meryet stopped him with a hand on his wrist.

"Gods have mercy on me," she laughed, "but you are in the presence of the Great Royal Wife, Nehesi. Show *some* decorum, please."

"Apologies, Great Lady."

"I swear by Mut, the two of you quarrel like you're married; you may as well be."

"You ought to come back inside, Great Lady," Batiret said. "The night is chill, and you need sleep for the festival tomorrow."

"She is right," Nehesi murmured. "The first day of the new year is always a long one. Plenty of sleep would suit you well tonight."

Meryet hooked her arm through Nehesi's elbow, pulled Batiret close with her other arm, clutching the woman in an affectionate hug. "Quarrel like an old married couple, and order me about like two overprotective parents. Oh, very well. Take me to my bed and tuck me in."

They did just that, Batiret marshaling the usual small army of body servants to take Meryet's wig and jewels, wash the paint from her face and soothe her skin with a cool cream. They dressed her in a fine silk night-robe – a gift from Thutmose, from his store of costly foreign fabrics – and eased her into her bed with soft voices, quiet music, the low flicker of a single wick burning in her brass lamp.

Meryet, though, could not sleep. Rest evaded her, slipping beyond her grasp no matter how she turned on the mattress, no matter how she tilted the ivory cradle of her head-rest. After a time, the gentle, monotonous tones of the harpist became annoying, yet the thought of dismissing the woman seemed somehow cruel. She closed her eyes and lay quite still, feigning sleep until the harpist dismissed herself and the last of her body servants snuffed the lamp's wick. When she withdrew through the servants' door, Meryet was left alone with the sound of her own breathing and the faint, desultory crackle of the wick settling back into the oil.

A new year, she mused, shifting against her head-rest. *And a new battle for Thutmose. I have no reason to think it's so, and yet I do. Why?*

She opened her eyes, watched through the pillars of the wall as the sycamore swayed in the wind. It painted a shifting web of starlight and shadow over the gaps between the pillars. Sopdet, dominating the deep blue of the heavens, seemed to catch sight of her between the mobile black branches. Its stare was direct and forcefully bright.

Meryet raised her arms before the great statue of Waser. The golden discs sewn along the edge of her fine white winter shawl chimed with the movement.

"O Waser, holy one, originator, thou who make the dead live again! O Waser, Lord of Silence, thou who art forever kind and young! Thy wife Iset comes to thee in love. She has reassembled thee; she has raised thee up; she has opened thy mouth, that the breath of life might fill thy nostrils again. Exhale the breath of life across our land!"

The god gazed over her head, smiling impassively at the crowd of nobles gathered at her back. The statue was more than twice the height of a man, his skin painted as green as a fertile field. The black jut of a conical beard pointed outward from his stern face, but his smile was benign, nearly loving, and his eyes were, Meryet thought, as warm as stone eyes could be.

Beside her, Thutmose bore the offering tray, a great silver platter heaped with green offerings of every kind: bundles of herbs, the pliant branches of young trees, sheaves of still-unripe wheat, and a pyramid of several kinds of fruit, which Thutmose took the greatest care not to upset. It would never do to have the New Year's offerings go tumbling down the steps and into the crowd.

Sleep had evaded Meryet the night before the ceremonies. Eventually she had risen to walk again in her garden, but the chill had soon driven her back beneath the blankets. She had drifted in and out of consciousness, her body sometimes giving an involuntary jerk of exhaustion that pulled her cruelly back from the verge of true restful sleep. When the dawn broke and the birds chorused outside, she was relieved to rise from the bed and cast all hope of sleep aside. It was futile, and Meryet did not enjoy pursuing futility.

She had at least been spared walking the long road to the temples at Ipet-Isut. A litter had carried her, and she had ridden it uncomfortably, fighting the urge to rub at her stinging, tired eyes. She pushed her way through the ceremonies of the Opening of the Year with dogged focus, promising herself that there would be time for a nap between ceremony and feast. Strange, that the surety of returning to her bed, the very site of her night-long torment, should be all that kept her from breaking into hysterical laughter or sobs of frustration now, before the eyes of the gods and the court.

The invocation of Waser was the final phase of the Opening of the Year. *Only a few moments more, and I will be on my litter returning to Waset. Gods, but I'm tired!*

She reached for the bundle of herbs on Thutmose's tray, held it aloft for Waser to inspect.

There was an abrupt sound in the crowd behind her, a stifled exclamation of surprise. Meryet ignored it, and went on with her intonations to the god.

As she lifted the sheaf of wheat over her head, a wider murmur came from the crowd, and something that sounded like a whimper of fear. Meryet glanced quickly over her shoulder. Her eyes went immediately, instinctively, to where Amunhotep's nurse stood. The woman was there, and the prince too. In fact, the nurse held him clutched tightly to her breast, though at nearly four years of age, Amunhotep was old enough to stand on his own at the front of the crowd. In that brief moment, as Meryet glimpsed the nurse's face, she saw in the woman's dark eyes and compressed lips the trace of fear, as well as ferocious determination.

What in the name of the gods...?

As Meryet turned back to Waser, her eye passed swiftly over another woman's face – Amenemhat's nurse, pale, eyes wide, mouth open in an expression of panic. Her arms were empty.

Meryet paused with the sheaf of wheat raised above her head. "Thutmose," she whispered urgently. Her voice barely carried beyond the braids of the wig that framed her face, hiding it at this angle from the eyes of the nobles. "Something is wrong."

Thutmose's eyes shifted, but he did not upset his pyramid of fruits. "What is it?"

"The boys' nurses."

Thutmose, too, glanced quickly over his shoulder. When he returned his eyes to the god, Meryet could see grim understanding paling his features. "Where is Amenemhat?"

Meryet gave the dedication of the wheat as quickly as propriety would allow, and, in the act of turning to the tray to lift the sapling branches, she allowed her eyes to run over the crowd. Nehesi was ushering Amenemhat's nurse from the temple, steering her with a firm hand.

"Just get through the ceremony," Meryet whispered. "Then we will know."

Meryet walked calmly back to her litter, her path strewn with bunches of herbs tossed by the watching crowd. She seized Batiret's hand as she mounted onto her chair, pulled the woman onto the litter's platform with her. The bearers lifted the platform into the air, and Batiret, unused to riding on the shoulders of men, squeaked where she crouched at Meryet's feet. She gripped the legs of the chair in white-knuckled fists.

Meryet leaned close. "What in Amun's name happened back there?"

"Gods preserve me, Great Lady. Satiah's boy – Amenemhat – he's gone."

"What?"

Scores of nobles, to say nothing of the crowds of rekhet in their festival best, lined the long road from Ipet-Isut to Waset's palace. Meryet struggled to keep her face calm.

"His nurse lost sight of him, and he...he vanished. Nehesi took her out of the temple before she could scream, and he set all his guards to work searching for the boy."

Meryet glanced about her. For the first time in over three years, Nehesi was not slinking along beside her. She had lost her shadow. Her eyes went unbidden to the scars on Batiret's arm, and Meryet shuddered. She willed panic out of her heart, pressing it away with the deliberate hand of her ka. She *ordered* it away.

"I am sure Nehesi's men will find the boy."

"Oh, gods," Batiret moaned. "It's Satiah – you know it is!"

"Stop this at once," Meryet hissed. "You are too sensible to behave this way."

Batiret breathed deeply, fighting against her own memories, her own terrors.

Meryet dropped her hand to the woman's shoulder and gave a quick, reassuring squeeze. "It will be well, Batiret. But you must keep your wits about you. I need you now."

"Ah, Great Lady."

The moment her litter arrived at Waset, Meryet exchanged it for another – a curtained one, so she might hide from public view. She and Batiret rode at once to the House of Women. The wailing, panicked shrieks of Amenemhat's nurse greeted Meryet in the courtyard; they sped to the boy's small room. The stricken nurse was at the center of a knot of frantic women. Her face was an ugly mess of red flush and wet black kohl.

"Here now," Meryet said, pushing into the crowd. Dimly, she was aware that Satiah might be in that crowd, Satiah and her knife, with Nehesi nowhere to be found. But she could not spare a worry for that now. She must find out what had happened to the boy. "Here now, Lady. Listen – listen to me! The Great Royal Wife stands before you. Take hold of yourself!"

The nurse did take hold of herself with visible effort, gulping back her tears, twisting the edge of her shawl between shaking hands.

"Tell me what happened," Meryet demanded.

The nurse could enlighten her no more than Batiret had. It seemed one moment the boy was there, and the next he was gone, and nowhere to be found.

"It must have been one of the priests." The sudden deep, masculine voice turned every woman's head, and in a moment the harem women were falling away in deep bows, murmuring *Lord Horus* and *King*. Meryet stared up into Thutmose's face, desperate, absurdly grateful to see him here, a rock in the midst of this chaotic, helpless current.

Thutmose nodded a tense greeting. "I figured somebody would bring the poor nurse back here to Amenemhat's room, though it probably does her no good to see it. Meritamun," he called into the crowd, and a tall, slender woman bowed at his shoulder. "Take this poor mawat to the kitchen and give her some strong wine. It will be all right," he added to the nurse as she went stumbling by, tucked under Meritamun's arm. "We will find your boy."

He sent the rest of the women away – all but Batiret, who remained stoically at Meryet's shoulder, grim and silent.

"You think it was a priest?" Meryet asked when they were alone.

"Or a priestess. Who else could move unnoticed at the edge of a festival crowd, and who else knows the temple well enough to whisk a child away unseen? Whoever took Amenemhat is hiding with him in some passage, some storeroom...."

"Nehesi's men are searching the temple now."

"Nehesi should not have left you," Thutmose said.

"I've survived. Let us worry about Amenemhat. Are you sure..." Meryet gave Batiret an apologetic glance, "...that Satiah herself didn't take the boy?"

"I am certain Satiah is still at her estate. I receive reports daily. The usual messenger arrived just as my litter returned to Waset, before I came here. She is...at her home."

"It's where they'll take the boy – whoever abducted him. They will bring him directly to Satiah."

"I know."

"You must go to her, too, Thutmose. You must get him back." Meryet's voice dropped to a whisper. "She is making her move. Now. She is reaching out for your throne."

"She will not take it," Thutmose vowed.

He turned on his heel and strode from the room. Meryet was left alone, clutching both of Batiret's hands in her own, the two of them standing wordless and frightened among the discarded playthings of Satiah's boy.

CHAPTER SEVENTEEN

THUTMOSE'S FASTEST SHIP LANDED AT the estate's moorings less than an hour later. He had traveled under sail and oar both, moving at all speed, the prow churning the water, the oars slapping the Iteru with a furious rhythm that sent white spray flying. A stiff wind had blown steadily, hurrying him south as if the gods themselves understood his urgency. And yet his progress still felt too slow. He glanced nervously at the sun's position in the pale winter sky as he leapt from the ship's deck to the crumbling stone quay.

He had no guard with him now – none but the guards who waited at the estate itself. Thutmose ran up the long roadway, past fields long since harvested, their earth dry and bare, shot with the dun tufts of winter weeds. He sprinted through the olive orchard where last season's leaves clung to tired branches. When he reached the hill that rose to the house, he slowed, mindful of his strength. It would not do to arrive in Satiah's presence winded and trembling. As he climbed, his hand stayed firmly on the hilt of his sword.

The guards had seen him coming, of course, and the gate stood open to him, flanked by bowing men. The small, tidy garden was empty, silent and breathless, crouched as if waiting for him to strike a great and terrible blow.

Thutmose marched toward the dark arch of Satiah's doorway. The scent of fresh myrrh smoke reached him before the darkness of her chambers closed across his vision.

"Satiah," Thutmose called harshly.

She made no answer, but as his eyes grew accustomed to the dark, a small, pale form asserted itself against the blackness. Satiah was perched like a tiny, delicate bird on an ebony chair. Its back was high, ornately carved. Her hands lay on arm rests very like those on Thutmose's own throne. In the dimness of her chamber, half-lit by the offering bowl burning at her small Hathor shrine, she looked as grim and powerful as any Great Royal Wife who had ever ruled from the dais in the Hall of Audiences.

Thutmose advanced on her. "Where is the boy?"

She held up a hand imperiously, and without thinking, Thutmose stalled. He cursed himself for capitulating like a subject.

"Tell me where he is, Satiah, and I'll spare your life."

"Spare my life? You did not come to kill me, Thutmose."

"Where?"

"Amenemhat is not here."

"I don't believe you."

She shrugged.

"How did you contrive to take him? And at a ceremony, Satiah! I never would have thought *you* would defile a holy day."

"It defiles nothing, for a child to be with his mother. It is you who offends the gods – you who cast me off unjustly and put a false Great Royal Wife in my place."

"Unjustly? You murdered Senenmut and crushed your own mother's heart."

Satiah's eyes narrowed. "My mother," she said. Her voice, weighted with equal stones of loathing and calculation, sank into the pit of Thutmose's stomach.

"It must have been somebody in the temple who took him," Thutmose growled. "It certainly was not you. You hadn't the time to return here before I arrived. Tell me who did it, and how it was done."

"Or what?" said Satiah lightly. "Or you'll kill me?"

"Do not try me. You have long since gone beyond your boundaries, *Satiah*. You forget that I am the Pharaoh."

"Pharaohs do not live forever."

Thutmose reached out in the darkness, seized her by the front of her gown. He jerked her to her feet, and light and small as she was, she stumbled in his grip. He pulled her face close to his; the dark daggers of her eyes stabbed into his own. "Tell me where."

"The boy is not here," Satiah said calmly. "Disbelieve me if you must; it will not change the truth."

Thutmose released her gown as if it had burned him. She dropped back onto her ungilded throne. He shouted through the courtyard for Djedkare; in moments the soldier arrived, saluting with his palms outstretched.

"Summon half your men. They are to search every crack and corner of this property. Not even the smallest box is to be left unopened. If anyone comes from the quay – or from any direction – tell me at once."

"Ah, Mighty Horus."

"Search all you please," Satiah hissed. "You will not find my son. He is not yours to control. He belongs to the gods, as do I."

Thutmose ignored her. He joined in the efforts of his men, kicking open doors to tiny side rooms, upending baskets of dried fruit, tearing clothing from cedar chests.

He knew he would not find the boy. It was his rage he served. As he ravaged each corner of her home, the fire in his ka was both quenched and fed. He hated himself for his own weakness, his fear of Satiah's power. He loathed his own inaction against the Retjenu as Hatshepsut lay dying, the months he had spent on campaign as his son grew without him, as his wife ruled without him. Most of all, he despised himself for being human – for having no power to halt the gods' plots. Even as Pharaoh, he could do nothing to ease Hatshepsut's suffering. Even as Pharaoh, he could not erase his own past. He knew it was the action of a child, to lash out impotently at objects and take a thrill in their destruction, to feel power over the ruin he made. But Thutmose did not care.

Satiah sat imperturbable on her dark throne, staring straight ahead as Thutmose and his soldiers turned her neat home to a refuse heap. Her face was an emotionless mask. She did not deign to notice the fury of the king until he stood over her Hathor shrine, staring down at the seven little statues of the goddess arranged around their smoking bowl of myrrh. He eyed the shrine with the current of rage rising beneath his heart.

"Don't dare touch it," Satiah said. Her voice grated harshly in her throat.

Thutmose dismissed his men from his presence. They made their way briskly past the piles of torn linen, the strewn cushions, the upended wicker couch. When they had gone, he met her hard, dark eyes. The depth of hatred in her stare sent a tremble of loathing through his body. To think that he had once lusted after her, had once hungered for her body as a starving man hungers for bread. A bitter foulness rose on his tongue. He would have spat it out onto her polished floor, had his mouth not been so dry.

"Don't presume to tell the Pharaoh what he may and may not touch."

"The Pharaoh," Satiah said, mockery ringing in her high voice. "Should I fear your title? The title of a mere man?"

Thutmose clenched his jaw and his fists. Her words struck too near the doubts of his own heart. "I do not need to remind you, of all people, of my divinity."

"Perhaps you need reminding of *my* divinity, dear brother. I have been consecrated by my union with the gods. Egypt is mine to give to my son. I cannot fail; the gods will not allow me to fail. Amenemhat will have the throne, as is right for one born of divinity. I will serve the gods beside him. You and yours will be cast aside like the weak, human-bred flotsam you are. It will come to pass. It cannot be halted."

"I should kill you for such treasonous speech."

"And yet you will not. My son's inheritance has been promised me by a power far greater than your own. You saw for yourself how the gods' own servants do the work I set before them, and with glad hearts. They are eager to serve me. Even at Ipet-Isut, the priests know I am divine, and turn their hands to my holy tasks."

"You're mad."

"I am blessed. Doubly blessed – not only by my union with the gods, but by my birth. You, Mighty Horus, are the son of a dancing girl and a weak boy, for all the royal trappings you wear. I am of the blood of Amun."

"*Neferure* was of the blood of Amun. You are Satiah, as you have insisted before."

"There are those who know who I was before – before I was consecrated. There are those who remember."

"Like the priest who stole Amenemhat away?"

She smiled coldly. "And more."

If she was prepared to shed her disguise and marshal an army of priests against him, then Satiah's madness had grown far greater than Thutmose had feared. She had made her living, in those long months after her escape, working her way through temples. And not only the temples of Amun, but of Min, Iset, Sobek, Hapi...her influence, for all Thutmose knew, could be vast. He had made no serious missteps as Pharaoh; his subjects had no reason to rejoice in his deposition. But if the priests of the Two Lands believed her claim stronger than his own – if they believed her claim more divine than his own.... She had already worked sufficient influence on at least one member of the priesthood, had convinced at least one man or woman to risk life and station by abducting Amenemhat from under the Pharaoh's holy nose, and in the midst of a ceremony, no less. Thutmose realized with a chill that these reins had slid far out of his grasp long ago. He was riding a careening chariot pulled by a mad horse, with no way to stop it or to influence its frantic, wild-eyed path.

In his desperate rage, in his helplessness, Thutmose did the only thing that made sense. He lifted his foot and placed it against the low tabletop of Satiah's shrine. Her eyes widened in sudden panic. Thutmose kicked out with all the force of his fury. The seven aspects of Hathor went tumbling across the floor; burning myrrh spilled across the tiles. Satiah shrieked, threw herself to her knees among the smoldering embers. She seized one of the toppled statues and clutched it to her chest, gasping, rocking it as if it was a child she had snatched from the jaws of a crocodile. She turned her blazing eyes on Thutmose, rendered mute by her hatred.

"You will not win, Neferure. The throne will never be yours, no matter what I must do to keep you in your place."

Chapter Eighteen

MERYET ROSE EXPECTANTLY FROM HER couch when she heard the low, urgent conversation of her servants outside her chamber door. She knew the message they bore before she admitted them: the Pharaoh had returned. Her women bowed low when Nehesi opened the scarab-carved doors of her chambers, and plump Hemetre said breathlessly, "Mighty Horus is in his chambers, Great Lady."

"Take me there."

Batiret and Hemetre accompanied her, following the train of her festival gown, a floating gauze of green linen to honor Waser and the New Year. Jewels and gold hung heavily at her throat, her wrists, her ankles. She felt so weighted by ceremony and expectation that it was a wonder she could sweep through the halls of the palace as quickly as she did, with head high and gaze steady. Her heart's beat was certainly not steady; it fluttered in her chest like a bird dodging the strike of a tree-snake.

Nehesi clapped to announce her arrival at the Pharaoh's doors. Even through the barrier of limestone wall and cedar door, she heard the weariness, the bewilderment in Thutmose's voice. "Come."

He sat on one of his lovely couches, elbows on knees, hands dangling useless between his legs. Thutmose stared into the shadow of the niche below his windcatcher, watching the wine jars cooling there with a dull, distant expression.

149

"Thutmose."

He looked up at her, blinked at her finery as though her brightness and beauty were some incantation that muddied his senses. He still wore the simple kilt and plain wig he had donned when he'd flown to Satiah's estate.

"The Feast of the New Year begins in an hour," she reminded him. "You can't go looking like this." Meryet clapped for his body servants, and they came scrambling from their small adjoining chambers. "Make the Pharaoh ready for the feast," she commanded, her voice far harder and more impatient than she would have liked.

They dispersed to gather his finery from his chests and dressing tables, and Meryet dropped onto the couch beside him. "What happened, my love?"

"The boy was not there."

Meryet nodded, unsurprised. It had been too much to hope, that it could be so simple, that Satiah would play into Thutmose's hands with such ease. The woman was mad, it was true – but she was also no fool.

"Nehesi's men couldn't find him in the temple, either," Meryet admitted. "Nor anywhere in the palace. They are still looking, of course, but…"

Thutmose shook his head. "It makes no difference. She is already making her bid for the throne."

"She can't!"

"She revealed her true identity to at least some of the priests in the temple – why else would they have dared to take the boy? No priest would have crossed the Pharaoh for a mere Lady Satiah. But for Neferure, the daughter of Hatshepsut, who was the son of Amun himself…."

Meryet's hands felt suddenly cold. "But Thutmose, you have been an ideal king. The priests have no reason to try to depose you."

He threw up his hands. "I can think of no reason, but

the gods alone know what she's told them. Clearly, Meryet, someone at the temple is under her influence. And if one man, why not a dozen? If a dozen, why not a hundred, or a thousand? Kings have been pulled down by conspiracies before. Even good kings."

Meryet took his hand in her own, hoping to lend him some courage. But her hand shook.

"By Amun," Thutmose growled. "I've been so preoccupied with the rebellion in Kadesh, and before that, Hatshepsut's illness. I neglected Satiah; I didn't watch her closely enough."

"How under Re's light did she manage to communicate with the temple? She never left that estate."

"I don't know. I have turned it over and over in my heart, but I can't puzzle it out. This is exactly like the first time I had her. She escaped from her cell then, and I never knew out how she did it. She says the gods spirited her away."

An uneasy silence fell between them. At last Meryet ventured, "Do you believe it?"

"No," he said. "Never. There is some other explanation, for all of it. She is mad, not divine. And I will not allow a madwoman to conspire against me."

"That hound has already been loosed," Meryet said quietly. "Now we must find some way to leash it again."

"Lord Horus?" One of Thutmose's men bustled out of the royal bedchamber, the fine white length of a formal kilt draped across his arms.

"The feast," Thutmose muttered, annoyed. "Gods, but there is nothing I feel less like doing now than feasting."

"It is expected," Meryet said apologetically. "I can think of no way out of it. And believe me, I have tried."

"I had best get dressed, then," Thutmose said, rising slowly.

The clatter of running feet sounded outside the apartment door, and the next moment, Thutmose's door guard shouted a challenge. Thutmose and Meryet shared a nervous glance. The urgency of a clap carried through the door. Thutmose nodded for his servant Hesyre to see to it.

"Please, old brother," said a man's voice, panting and puffing. "I must see the Pharaoh. It's of the greatest urgency."

"Let him in," Thutmose said.

Meryet clutched at her own fingers, her hands working into a painful knot. A man dressed in the blue-and-white striped kilt of a royal guard stumbled into the chamber and fell on his face before the king, stretching his hands along the ground in frantic subjugation.

Thutmose waved an impatient hand. "Get up, man. What is it?"

"The Lady Satiah, Mighty Horus. She's gone."

Meryet sprang to her feet, gripped Thutmose's arm. "Blessed mother Mut," she whispered, never knowing whether she spoke to Thutmose or to her own panicked ka. "She is coming here. The feast – the court."

"*How did she get free?*" Thutmose shouted.

"Please, Good God." The guard cringed on the floor. "Be merciful to your loyal servants. We are investigating – Djedkare is working tirelessly to find out. But we do not yet know."

"She is coming here, Thutmose," Meryet said. "To...to *reveal herself* before the entire court."

"By Set's red blood, she is *not*. Let her try."

"We've been so foolish," Meryet said close to his ear, her voice pitched low. "We should have killed her long ago."

"Nehesi," Thutmose shouted. "Put every guard you can find in the palace on the feast hall's doors. The kitchen doors, too. The entire wing is to be patrolled. The Lady Satiah is not to set one foot inside that hall. She is to be apprehended on first sight and brought to me."

"As you say, Lord Horus." Nehesi dodged from the chamber, intent as a falcon on his task.

Thutmose sent the estate guard back to his post with a message of encouragement for Djedkare and his men. Then he turned to Meryet, took her hands in his own. He kissed her knuckles. "She cannot be in Waset yet. The travel time from the estate – even if she has access to a boat, it would take her an hour or more to get here. Go back to your chambers. I will send Nehesi to you the moment he's arranged the guard on the hall."

"But what shall we do? The feast..."

"It must go on, as if nothing is amiss. We mustn't allow her to disrupt the court in any way. Can you be brave, my lioness?" His fingers brushed her cheek. "I know you can. I know you are the true Great Royal Wife, whatever that twisted creature might think."

"Amunhotep..."

"Is safe, and so are you."

"Very well," Meryet said, her voice quavering. "I will be brave."

She collected her women outside Thutmose's door. Hemetre's round face was flushed, her eyes wide with barely controlled fear. Batiret looked calmer, but her pale face was tinged a sickly green shade around the mouth. She glanced about her continually as they made their way back to Meryet's chambers, as if she feared what might lurk in the shadows of the pillars.

For Meryet's part, never had walking sedately through the palace colonnades and courtyards seemed such an impossible task. Her legs shook; she feared she might collapse with every step. Her heart throbbed painfully in her throat. But the gods were good to her; somehow she managed to breathe, and restrained herself from running. Any of the servants they passed, any foreign dignitary or noble woman fanning herself under the shadow of a vined porch, might be Satiah's creature.

Meryet gave none of them the satisfaction of seeing fear on her face. She was, after all, the Great Royal Wife, whatever schemes the creeping spider Satiah might be weaving.

Her wing of the palace appeared around the bend of an outer hall cast half in bright light and half in sinister blue-black shade. She found Batiret's hand and squeezed it. They had made it to their sanctuary unharmed.

Meryet slipped through her scarab doors with her two women beside her and shoved the doors closed, leaning her back against them in relief, her eyes shut tight against her anxiety. "Oh, gods," she moaned.

The rustle of several linen gowns answered her. Meryet's eyes snapped open. Several women sank into deep bows in her antechamber; in the frantic heartbeats before she recognized them, she thought a small, vengeful army of Satiahs had arrived before her, appearing under the power of the dark gods she served like a mist above the river. Then she pressed her hands hard against her roiling belly, and with relief so vast it nearly dropped her to the tiles of her floor, she knew the women. Meritamun, Khuit, and Henuttawy – women of Thutmose's harem.

"Mut preserve me! Ladies, why are you here?"

They straightened, and Meryet saw the confusion and fear clouding their eyes. *Satiah, of course.*

"So she went to the harem," Meryet mused aloud. "We thought she would appear at the feast, but it's the House of Women she seeks to control next. Is that the way of it?"

It made sense, after all. The House of Women was a chest full of living jewels: daughters of Egypt's finest and most influential families. It was a subtler and more politically astute maneuver than barging into a feast like a gout of leaping flame.

"Great Lady," Meritamun stammered. The tall woman was still bent double in a subservient bow. "We beg your forgiveness for coming to you like this. Your women let us in when they understood the urgency of our errand."

"It's all right. Rise, all of you. Tell me."

Henuttawy spoke up. Her voice, usually light and musical with the practiced charm of a harem favorite, was strangled and ugly now. "*She* appeared, Great Lady. We thought her dead. The King's Daughter – Neferure."

"She is not dead," said Meryet, quite unnecessarily. Her tongue was sluggish and thick in her mouth.

"She had a child with her," Khuit said. "A boy. She told us the boy is her son and the true heir to the throne."

Meryet's heart worked feverishly to piece together this riddle. Thutmose had said it would take Satiah an hour by boat to travel from the estate. She must have left just after Thutmose had departed, and sailed directly for the House of Women. Somewhere along the way she met with the priest who had snatched Amenemhat from the temple that morning. This was a carefully orchestrated plot, well-crafted over many weeks. What other paths had Satiah paved for herself, what roads had she laid into the hearts of Egypt's great houses, into the temples and priesthoods?

The women's words tumbled over one another now, so eager were they to spill out the story.

"She said the boy is the son of the gods..."

"...demanded that those women who are loyal to the gods bring their families into line..."

"...she wanted us to swear our support to her cause. Imagine!"

"...after what she did to Batiret. We are no fools; we remember."

Meryet raised a hand for silence. "Did any women swear to her cause?"

The women looked uneasily at one another, but none spoke.

Meryet choked back a curse. "Who? I need to know which noble houses are backing Sati...Neferure. Immediately."

"We don't know, in truth," Meritamun said quickly. "We left for the palace as soon as we understood what she was about."

"But many of the women do fear her," Khuit supplied. "You see, Great Lady, when she lived among us she had a...a reputation."

"A reputation?"

"For great power."

"For great strangeness," Henuttawy said with a snort. "That woman is mad as a donkey with a wasp in its ear."

"Some of the women believe Neferure is not mad, but has the powers of a great priestess," Khuit said. "They believe she has magic nearly as great as the magic of the gods themselves."

"She is the daughter of Hatshepsut, after all," said Meritamun quietly. "And Hatshepsut..."

"Was of the blood of Amun," Meryet snapped. "I *know*."

Meritamun ducked her head in apology.

"Listen, all of you," Meryet insisted, hoping her words were true even as she said them. "This isn't magic. She had friends – people in her service, foul insects to carry her messages for her, to assist her in weeks' worth of plotting." *One of the guards at the estate, obviously. One or more. And who else? Might one of these very women be in Neferure's control?*

"In any case, Great Lady," Henuttawy said with a self-conscious glance in Batiret's direction, "we all know Neferure can be dangerous and unpredictable. Confronted with her that way, suddenly and so unexpected, as if she had returned from the tomb, there is no telling which women might capitulate to her demands. We knew we had to tell you at once."

"You did well," Meryet said. "Batiret, is Nehesi back yet?"

Batiret, still pressed silently against the chamber door, shook her head. "Not yet, Great..."

A woman's harsh scream filled the hallway beyond. Batiret leapt away from the door as if it had scalded her skin. The scream came again, rising, keening, curdling the blood in Meryet's veins.

She stood stricken for a long moment as the cry filled her ears. Then it filled her heart, and she realized from where it came.

Amunhotep's room.

Meryet wheeled, seized the handles of her massive double doors. She threw them open onto a scene of panic spilling into the hallway from her son's chamber.

Chapter Nineteen

Amunhotep's nurse reeled from the open door of the child's nursery, her hands flailing at the air. Her eyes were as wide as the eyes of a sacrificial bull in the moment when the knife drops to its neck. Nehesi charged down the hall toward the nurse, calling harshly for order. Beyond him, Thutmose ran from the direction of his chambers, his kilt and wig flying, his mouth set into a grim line.

Meryet reached the nurse a moment before the others did. She caught the woman in her arms, shouting into her ear, striving desperately to restrain her. She did not want to look into Amunhotep's chamber. She feared what she might find.

Nehesi and Thutmose took hold of the nurse, pulled her waving, clawing hands to her sides. Meryet was dimly aware of more women crowding around, all of them dressed in the finery of the House of Women. So Thutmose, too, had received messengers from the harem, carrying news of Satiah's startling appearance.

"He's gone," the nurse wailed. "Gone!"

Meryet loosed the nurse, staggered to Amunhotep's door. The boy's little bed stood vacant in the center of the room.

A scream twice as loud and desperate as the nurse's ripped from Meryet's throat.

"How did this happen?" Thutmose bellowed as Meryet sagged. A pair of familiar arms caught her before she could fall; she buried her face against Batiret's neck, keening her shock.

"Oh, gods," the nurse cried. "I only turned my back for a moment. I had dressed the little prince for the feast, and he fussed for his favorite toy, so I stepped out into the garden to fetch it. And when I returned he was gone – just *gone!*"

Nehesi shoved past Meryet into the nursery. She peered after the old guardsman, her thoughts clouded by terror. As she watched, Nehesi seemed to move through the room with the slow, dragging motions of a man underwater. The interior door that connected the nurse's sleeping chamber to the prince's was closed, but it was the only possible ingress. Any person who entered through the main door, where Meryet now huddled with her fan-bearer, would have been spotted at once by Meryet's guards.

Nehesi moved into the nurse's chamber, scouring for evidence. He let himself out by the side entry, further down the hall. From where Meryet stood, the side entry was partially blocked by the edge of a pillar. It may just have been possible for one of Satiah's creatures to enter the room there, unnoticed by the guards.

Thutmose was questioning those same guards, one finger stabbing toward their cringing faces.

"It was a palace servant," Meryet said, steadying herself with a ferocious effort. "Or someone dressed as a palace servant."

Thutmose rounded on her. "What?"

"A palace servant. Think, Thutmose: they are all but invisible. These men never would have taken note of a servant going about her duties with her head down."

"It is their responsibility to take note."

"Put them in custody if you like and question them later. Doing it now won't get our son back!"

"The nurse is lucky she was out in the garden when it

happened, Lord," Nehesi said quietly. "Whoever was sent in through her chamber door would have been armed. Had the nurse been present, she would not have survived."

"Had she been present, my son might be in his bed right now!" Thutmose pressed the heels of his hands against his eyes. "You're right, of course, Meryet. We need to get Amunhotep back – *now*. The rest we will sort out after he's returned to us safely."

"Alert the entire palace, Lord," Nehesi suggested. "Guests are arriving from all over Waset for the feast. Turn all their eyes to your service. The abductor won't go far if every noble and lady of Waset is looking for the prince."

"A good plan. Do it, Nehesi."

"No," Meryet cried. Her limbs shook violently; whatever shreds of clam she had summoned abandoned her. She wanted to run screaming down the hall, tearing at the pillars with her nails and teeth until the stone of the palace yielded up Amunhotep and the foul beast who had taken him. She drew a deep breath. "Send someone else. I want Nehesi here with me."

It was the harem women who went to spread the word. Eager to be of some service in such a fearful time, they raced through the palace, shouting the alert. Soon pillars and courtyard walls echoed with the sounds of running feet, the voices of men and women calling, "*Amunhotep! Prince!*"

Thutmose gathered Meryet in his arms.

"Gods, Thutmose," she cried, pressing her face against his chest. "It's madness. The whole palace is in an uproar. This is exactly what she wanted."

"It will help us find our son."

Meryet willed herself to think clearly. "She was at the House of Women only a short time ago."

"And she will be meeting up with whoever took Amunhotep somewhere between the harem and the palace. Unless..."

"Don't say it." Meryet did not want to think it, but she could not banish the terrible possibility from her lurching heart. Satiah had come to clear the way for Amenemhat's ascension to the throne. It meant death for Meryet's own sweet son.

"He's alive," Thutmose murmured. "Nehesi is right – whoever came through that nurse's door had to be armed, to dispatch any opposition to their Set-cursed task. If Satiah wanted our son dead, it would have been done in the nursery."

Meryet shuddered. *"Thutmose!"*

"He's alive, and we will find him somewhere between this place and the House of Women. I swear it."

"But where?" Meryet sobbed.

Waset was impossibly large, a great sprawl of humanity along the Iteru's eastern bank, filled with secretive passages, dark cellars, unknown alleys leading to the gods knew where. Beyond, the fields and rekhet villages were larger still, an endless, unsolvable maze stretching from north to south – and Meryet's only child could be anywhere, *anywhere!*

"The quay," Thutmose said. "The fastest route to the House of Women is by water." He paused, his eyes distant with thought. Then he said too quietly, too calmly, "No. No, she is not planning to bring her son to the palace, to present herself at the feast. We miscalculated."

"We've miscalculated all along!"

"The priest who took Amenemhat – don't you see?"

"No," Meryet cried desperately.

"Satiah's influence runs deep at the temple. She will take her son there first, to present him formally to the gods. She will go to receive the blessing of the priesthood, unopposed, while all of Waset is distracted by the feast. And she will take Amunhotep with her."

"How do you know? You can't know! We cannot afford another misstep, Thutmose – not now!"

"I know her," he said simply. "She is my sister."

The chariot raced along the abandoned road toward Ipet-Isut. The river already promised a bountiful flood, poised on the edge of the season of Akhet. To either side of the causeway the fields had begun to shimmer with the water that accumulated in every divot and furrow. Thutmose took it for encouragement, an assurance that the gods saw him, and would aid his cause against this enemy as they had done so many times before.

To his left, Nehesi handled the reins of the swiftest horses in Waset. To his right, Meryet clung grimly to the rail, her face falcon-fierce. Back in the palace she had summoned her courage and composure with a visible effort, but now that it was upon her she was as solid and cold as a statue of a warrior-goddess. Thutmose pulled his wife tight against his side and felt her tremble, for all her bravery. Or perhaps the shiver he felt was in his own flesh.

Ipet-Isut grew ever larger before them, its several temples and colossal statues seeming to drift apart as they came closer, to separate themselves like individual trees in the great forests of the far north. Somewhere in that maze of temples his sister moved like a malignant ghost, small and white and baleful. She would be there, waiting for him. Thutmose was sure of it.

The square outer gates of the complex passed overhead. The bulky forms of statues five times the size of a man flashed rapidly by, dizzying Thutmose with the speed of their passage. Nehesi slowed the horses as they gained the inner courtyard. Their hooves sounded loud and hollow on the paving stones, the echo rattling off the surrounding walls of temples and shrines like a pebble shaken inside an empty jar.

The horses halted, blowing, and Thutmose glanced around

the courtyard. A few apprentice priests scuttled forward to take the horses' reins, crouching into hasty bows as they ran. In the mouths of shrines, priestesses stretched their palms toward the king. He opened his mouth to demand of the people gathering in the courtyard where the Lady Satiah had gone, which temple hid her – and snapped his mouth closed with a click. He knew.

She is of the blood of Amun. She will take her son to Amun's shrine first. She must *be there!*

They ran up the steps to the Temple of Amun without a care for the priests looking on. The black mouth of the temple yawned above them, wide as the sky, waiting to swallow Thutmose and his wife, his son, his throne.

The umber dimness of the temple's interior closed in. Meryet pressed close to Thutmose's side. A single brazier stood alight far into its depths, near the door to the black inner sanctuary where the god lived. Thutmose squeezed Meryet's hand for reassurance, and together they made their way toward the fearsome star of that distant brazier.

A tight snake of apprehension coiled in Thutmose's gut. This was Amun's shrine they were about to enter, unpurified, without any offering save for their own fearful, desperate hearts. His lips move on a silent prayer, begging the god to forgive him. *Thou art the father of the gods, Lord Amun, the father of us all. How can I, a father, do anything but what I now do?*

He found Nehesi's grave eyes in the glow of the brazier, jerked his head toward the sanctuary. With a nod, Nehesi seized the handle and opened the door wide.

The light of the brazier spilled all at once into the sanctuary. A series of rapid impressions assaulted Thutmose's eyes, quick and flashing like lightning above the cliffs of Retjenu. He saw in a fluttering glance the golden feet, legs, knees of the god, rudely illuminated where he sat on his throne; a small figure in white linen rising from a crouch, turning; Satiah's beautiful pale face looking up at him, twisted in shock and anger; the braids of Meryet's wig lifting like a black bird's wings as she sprinted into the sanctuary, arms outstretched. And Amunhotep, tearing his hand away from Satiah's with a squeal, his little legs pumping as he fled into his mother's arms.

Amenemhat sat quietly on the stone floor beside his mother. A wide basin stood waiting at the feet of the god – the kind of basin used to collect blood offerings from ritual cattle. Nearby a knife shivered on the floor, and Thutmose realized with a sick horror that above the beating of his heart and the cries of his wife and son, the repeating metal echo of bronze on stone rang from the walls of the sanctuary.

Amun save me – she dropped it. The knife was in her hand when I opened the door. It was poised above my son.

Nehesi was already moving to apprehend Satiah, but Thutmose shouldered him aside. He seized her by the front of her dress himself, hauled her roughly away from basin and blade. She lost her feet and clung to his wrist, steadying herself. The touch of her hand chilled his skin.

"Tell me why I shouldn't kill you," Thutmose spat into her face.

She bore her teeth in an ugly, challenging grin.

The boy Amenemhat clambered to his feet and stood watching the scene soberly. Thutmose felt a rush of guilt, that he should brutalize the boy's mother before his very eyes. *Though the gods know she deserves it.*

"Nehesi, take the boy."

Amenemhat did not protest when the hulking guard lifted him as easily as he might have lifted a two-day-old pup.

"Unhand my son," Satiah said, her voice raw with hatred. "A worthless beetle like you is not fit to touch the child of the gods."

Thutmose shook her. "Keep your mouth shut, *Lady Satiah*."

A commotion erupted in the temple. Thutmose heard a

shout of dismay, then, "Gods preserve me, the door! The light! Somebody close the sanctuary door!"

He heard the advance of running feet on stone, and a cry of "Amun is defiled by light! Who is responsible for..."

An old man stumbled to the sanctuary door and stopped abruptly, wheezing deep in a chest that clattered with dozens of amulets. Thutmose did not need to look around to know that it was Hapuseneb, the High Priest of Amun.

"Good day, Hapuseneb," Thutmose said, biting off his words in a parody of courtly casualness.

The High Priest gave a quavering wail of dismay as he bowed. "Mighty Horus, I would never presume to interfere in your...your business, but I must beg you humbly, desperately, to close the door! The god is offended by light upon his skin; you know this, Great Lord!"

"Hapuseneb, take this child from my guard. I need Nehesi's hands free."

"You won't kill me," Satiah whispered. It was not a plea. There was not a hint of desperation or fear in her voice, only cold assurance.

"Kill?" Hapuseneb sputtered. "Please, Lord, not in the sanctuary!"

Nehesi shoved the little boy into Hapuseneb's arms, then, with a muttered apology, the guardsman turned the priest around bodily and marched him out of the sanctuary. "The Pharaoh's orders," Nehesi said. "Take the child away from this place. He should not see what is to come."

"Bring him back," Satiah called out. "He must receive Amun's blessing!"

"Amenemhat will be treated well," Thutmose said levelly. "Let that, at least, be some small comfort to you when you set your heavy heart on Anupu's scales. For your sins are too numerous; you have no hope of redemption in the afterlife, Neferure."

The name widened her eyes for a heartbeat. Then she narrowed them again in mockery. "Do you think you know the heart of Anupu, or of any other god, O great king?"

"Nehesi," Thutmose said, "your sword."

Nehesi hesitated. Thutmose looked to him expectantly, and saw a cloud of superstitious fear cross his face.

"Not here, Mighty Horus. I beg you. I have already...er... Amun's sanctuary has been defiled once in the past. As we are speaking of Anupu's scales and heavy hearts, I would just as soon not do it here, for the sake of my own hopes for an afterlife."

Thutmose jerked his head in a quick nod. He pulled Neferure from the sanctuary. She clawed at his wrist where it held the front of her dress; she kicked at his ankles. But he hauled her from Amun's presence, down the length of the temple, out into Re's righteous light. It fell brightly, painfully on the white limestone of the temple steps. A crowd of priests and priestesses had gathered, watching wide-eyed as Thutmose stood his captive roughly on her feet. A murmur of *Satiah* passed through the crowd like a distant wind.

She tugged at her dress, putting it back into order, and turned her face toward the temple servants. But when she spoke, her words were for Thutmose alone. "You know I tamed the bull. You know that mine is the blood of Amun. You know my powers. The throne was meant for me, for my child."

At the mention of the Bull of Min, the familiar lance of religious dread struck deep into Thutmose's heart. But he looked to Meryet, saw her cradling Amunhotep in her arms, her face stern, her eyes vengeful. He recalled the sound of the dropped knife ringing in the darkness of the shrine.

And at last, Thutmose's anger was far greater than his fear.

"I call upon Amun," Neferure shouted. "I call upon Hathor, my great mistress, the Lady of the West. Strike down the false rulers, O gods of Egypt; restore the Horus Throne to your righteous inheritors! Let all those who fear the gods hear my words, and restore the throne to the blood of Amun!"

Thutmose snapped his fingers at Nehesi. The man took Neferure by the shoulders and pushed her, still ranting, to her knees. The sword came flashing from Nehesi's belt, but before he could raise it, Thutmose stepped forward impulsively and took the hilt in his own hand.

Neferure continued to call upon the gods, but Thutmose, ignoring her words and the heat in her eyes, took hold of her hair, pulled her head back to expose her pale throat. She cried out to the gods – not to save her, but to strike down the false Pharaoh who kept her from her divine birthright, to wipe him from the earth, to destroy his family and all that he loved.

Never.

The blade bit deep, cutting off Neferure's passionate invocation, spilling a red flood down the steps of the Temple.

Chapter Twenty

A GREAT CLOUD OF DUST hung over Ipet-Isut for two days. The vast, pale column was visible from the rooftops of Waset; the people of the city gathered beneath their cloth sunshades and peered north, wondering at the strange sign. Thutmose, too, wiled away what time he could spare on the rooftop of his own quarters. From there, the highest point in Waset, he gazed down the distant road. It stretched along the land on its dark causeway, leading to the toy-like temples shadowed by the pillar of dust.

Thutmose knew it was not a sign – or at least, not a message from divinity. The cloud was all too earthly in its origins, stirred up by the constant tramping of scores of feet, hundreds of feet in the complex of Ipet-Isut, where priests stirred the bare yards as they paced in heated discussion, where priestesses danced endlessly to appease the gods.

He leaned his elbows on the rooftop parapet and scowled as the dust cloud shifted, giving small way to the nudge of a river wind. He had spent his entire life in fear of omens and portents, of hidden powers lurking beneath human skin. In the end, it all came down to a rush of blood down the temple steps and the hot metal of a blade in his hand.

A lifetime spent cowering in fear of the gods' signs, and now the only sign I need fear is there, hanging over Ipet-Isut. And it is made by men. It was the kind of ironic riddle that would have made Hatshepsut laugh. Thutmose wrestled back tears.

Two days had passed since the lifeless body of Lady Satiah had been carried to the embalming house to rest beneath the

169

salts. Two days since Thutmose had found Djedkare waiting on the Pharaoh's return with one of the estate guards, battered and bruised, in his custody. The man had fallen in love with the beautiful and vulnerable Satiah, Djedkare explained, and had assisted her in secret, carrying messages to Waset and Ipet-Isut, finally facilitating her escape dressed in the rekhet rags of an orchard worker. The man had provided her with a boat to make her way to the city. The man had lost his life along with his senses and his heart.

It was a man who helped her escape, Thutmose thought morosely. He really had believed that a god had lifted her out of the estate, like a breeze lifting a bit of seed fluff. He should have known better. He was a king, not a credulous fool.

"May we approach, Mighty Horus?" It was Meryet calling for him, beautiful and strong, the lioness of his house. She stood at the top of an outer stairway that led down into his garden. He gazed at her a moment, content for the space of a few heartbeats to forget everything – Neferure, the knife, the cloud of dust hanging over the temples – everything but that he loved her.

He nodded, waved his permission.

Meryet led the High Priest of Amun onto the rooftop. Hapuseneb was nearing old age, with deep lines around his eyes and a permanent cleft between his brows. He had become rather jowly and stout, and the amulets he wore on cords about his neck seemed to have multiplied in recent days.

"High Priest," Thutmose said in greeting.

Hapuseneb made the requisite bows, and the three of them stood together in silence, watching the dust cloud ripple in the sunlight. At last Thutmose asked for news from the temple, and Hapuseneb sighed.

"Much as it was yesterday, Great Lord. Word is spreading to nearby cities that Lady Satiah is dead, and factions arrive from other temples to speak in her favor. They are all small factions, it is true, but together they make a voice that grows louder by the hour."

"Do they know who she truly was?"

"They do. It seems a chosen few in the Temple of Amun knew her secret. She told them, or perhaps they recognized her from years before. The truth is out among the servants of the gods, and it has only increased their affection for her."

"She planned that," Meryet said quietly. "I swear it, she did. That woman was too clever by half."

"She may have planned it, indeed," Hapuseneb muttered. "In any case, word spreads that she was the heir of Hatshepsut."

"What of it?" said Meryet. "Hatshepsut did not die without a clear successor. Thutmose was the Pharaoh for as long she – *longer*. There is no reason to evict him from the throne."

"Ah, that is so, Great Lady, but they loved their Lady Satiah well, after all the time she spent at the various temples, all the devotion she showed. I believe her devotion to the gods was true, for all her faults and deceptions. They do not love her without reason."

Thutmose turned his scowl from the dust cloud to Hapuseneb. "You are the High Priest; command them to give this up. I will not abdicate to Neferure's son, nor will I make him my heir."

Hapuseneb bowed quickly. "Of course, Great Lord – of course! I have already begun making it known that it will be as you say – there is no place for Neferure's child in the succession. I am the High Priest, as you say, but I am the High Priest of *Amun*. I do not control the other priesthoods."

"The Amun priesthood is the most powerful in the land."

Hapuseneb nodded. "Just so, Great Lord. And yet, as I said, many small factions join their voices together, and the ear hears one mighty shout. There is only so much even the High Priest of Amun can do against all the other priesthoods of all the other gods. Look at that cloud, Lord. All those pacing feet, all those dancing women. The cloud will settle with time, but it will be a long while before her name or her child's claim to the throne are forgotten by Egypt's priests."

The cloud did settle, but the temples of Upper Egypt remained in turmoil.

Two weeks later, Thutmose lay face down on the stone bench in his bath, submitting to the massage Meryet and the royal physicians had prescribed to soothe his tension. His bath had been especially hot, the scraping afterward bracing. A mist of steam and herbal oils hung thickly in the room. The scent lulled him pleasantly; his eyes slid shut as the woman worked at the knots in his shoulders and back with miraculously clever hands.

Gradually a muffled confusion of voices pierced his calm. The bath woman hesitated in her work, distracted by the sound. Thutmose sighed, dismissed her, and toweled the oil from his body with his own hands. When he was dressed, he made his way through his apartments with reluctant feet dragging at the tiles. The voices came from beyond the door to his private chambers – from his anteroom. There was an urgency to the sound that made Thutmose regret having left his stone bench.

It was Meryet and her fan-bearer, the woman who always accompanied her through the palace halls. Hesyre fussed about them, pouring wine and engaging in polite if deferent conversation with the Great Royal Wife.

Ah, Mighty Horus," Hesyre said, catching sight of Thutmose. "With your permission, Great Lady, I shall leave you to the Pharaoh."

When he had gone, Meryet sprang to her feet. Her mask of courtly calm fell away, and a strange anguish twisted her features.

"Amunhotep..." Thutmose began, his heart straining at his chest.

Meryet shook her head. "He is safe and well."

"What is it, then?"

"Oh, Thutmose." She pressed her palms against her cheeks as if she might soothe away a fever that burned inside her. "It's the temples. All up and down the Iteru, to north and south. Riots. Fighting. The priesthoods of all the gods are breaking apart."

Thutmose had no need to ask why. Another question prodded at his heart. "Why was I not told directly?"

Meryet hung her head, and her eyes dimmed with an unspoken apology. "You have been overtaxed of late. I instructed the messengers to come to me first so that I could keep the worst of the news from you, to give you some respite."

"Meryet! If I had known sooner, perhaps I could have stopped this."

"The riots are new," she said hastily. "I brought you the news the moment I heard of them, I swear it. Before it was only...rumors. Messages about how many priests were throwing their support behind Amenemhat. As Hapuseneb said, they will eventually forget Neferure, and let this go. But rioting..."

"How bad is it?"

"A priest was killed today at the Temple of Min in Abedju. And in Iunet, somebody has set the grain stores at the Temple of Hathor afire."

"Fire? Death? Amun's eyes!"

Meryet bit her lip, then said, "There is more."

"*Excellent.*"

"Hapuseneb just sent me this note." She pulled a bit of papyrus from the blue silk sash at her slender waist. "He says a large faction has split at the Temple of Amun – nearly half the priesthood – and he fears he can no longer retain control. Thutmose…" Meryet's voice trailed away. Her face was pale; her lips trembled.

"We must…we must do *something* with Amenemhat," Thutmose stammered.

The fan-bearer, waiting obediently a few paces behind her mistress, clenched her fists but remained silent.

"Gods preserve a fool, but I cannot countenance taking the boy's life," Meryet cried. "He's only a boy, still just a baby!"

"I know," said Thutmose. "It seems too grave a thing, too dire a misstep. And I'm afraid we have put our feet afoul of the path already."

"Do you mean…Satiah?"

He nodded. "I acted in rage when I killed her, did it without thinking. And now we have riots in the temples – burning!"

"You did no wrong," Meryet insisted. "She would have killed our son. She very nearly did. She deserved to die."

"She was a creature of evil," he agreed. "Perhaps it was not her fault – life in the court, a life of duty to the throne – it twisted her, corrupted her heart and her ka. But she was still a creature of evil, however she arrived at that fate. Maat is better served without her. No, I don't mean she should have lived. I only mean the way I did it…*where* I did it…. It was a misstep."

"We must do something, before these factions spread, before their influence reaches into the noble houses."

Thutmose thought sadly of Amenehmat. The boy was quiet and sweet, easy for his nurses to care for, a good playmate for the prince. Even at his young age, a curious intelligence shone in the boy's eyes. The thought of snuffing out the fire in the lad's little heart, and only because his mother had been more scorpion than woman, sickened Thutmose to the seat of his ka.

"We must do something, I agree. And yet I cannot – *will* not harm Amenemhat."

"I know." Meryet's voice broke with some raw emotion Thutmose could not identify. It wavered somewhere between defeat and horror. Her hand fell to her side; the slip of papyrus drifted to the floor. "Thutmose," she said reluctantly, "I can think of one way to stop the riots."

"How?"

But she would not speak. Meryet stumbled to one of the silk-covered couches and sank onto it, pressing her hands against her stomach as if she might be ill. Batiret hovered nearby, biting her lip, frowning.

"How?" Thutmose said again. "Speak, Meryet."

"If Amenemhat is not of the blood of royalty," she said haltingly, "if he is not of the blood of Amun...then the priests will have no more cause to back him."

Thutmose shook his head, uncomprehending. His heart was shrouded in a thick fog of confusion and despair. He could glean no sense from Meryet's words. "But he *is* of Amun's blood. Through Hatshepsut..."

Batiret let out a cry of pain. Her hands flew to her mouth.

And in the same moment the fan-bearer grasped Meryet's terrible, impossible meaning, Thutmose grasped it, too, and wanted to throw it away from his conscience the way a farmer flings a cobra from his field, wanted to spit it from his mouth like the bitterest bile.

"Through Hatshepsut," he repeated hoarsely.

"No," Batiret sobbed, falling to her knees before Meryet, clinging to the hem of her gown. "I beg you, Great Lady. Do not do this. For the sake of what you and I shared between us, please..."

"Rise, Batiret," Meryet said quietly.

But Batiret pitched herself onto her face and lay keening

on the Pharaoh's floor.

"Batiret, please." Meryet stooped, pulled the woman onto the couch beside her with some difficulty. All the strength seemed to have gone out of the fan-bearer's bones like water from a dropped pail. She hung limp as an old doll in Meryet's grasp. Meryet bundled her into her arms and rocked her, murmuring comfort or excuses into the woman's ear.

"I believe you are right," Thutmose said. "There may be no other way."

"She told you once," Batiret howled, "she told you once not to put the throne before what is good, what is maat! I know she told you. I know you swore."

"Don't speak to the Pharaoh that way," Meryet said, but in spite of her admonishment there was a note of sympathy in her words.

But Thutmose did not heed the weeping woman's impertinence. Had his own heart not been stilled by the horror of what he contemplated, he would have fallen to the floor and wailed his grief, too. The sound of Hatshepsut's words came forcefully to his memory, that blue night in her garden when she had fallen into the grass, a king defeated by her own hand, and cursed all the gods.

Tell me you will not choose the throne over the things that truly matter – over family, over love. Over eternity.

And he had promised. *The gods curse me*, he thought angrily, then realized with a shiver of bitter humor that the gods had cursed him indeed. And would go on cursing him, and cursing him, striking him, confounding him. How could they do less? What else would a sin so enormous earn him, but the spite of the gods? Hatshepsut had said that she lived only in stone. It was truer now than it had been when she had still walked among the living. Her images on her monuments, her name encircled by the royal cartouche – these were the places where her kas now dwelt. If Thutmose erased her image and name from the land, her kas would lose their eternal homes and flee into darkness. She would be lost forever. Forgotten. She would be dead eternally.

But the throne would be safe. The riots would cease. Egypt would remain whole. And was that not the very thing Hatshepsut had worked for all her life, to keep Egypt whole?

Thutmose let his heart wander painfully, stumbling back to the blue night in the garden. He recalled with a pang of guilt the words he had told himself as he crouched in the wet grass beside the weeping king: *the Horus Throne is the legacy of our family. It is an unbreakable link to those who came before, to those who will come after, for generations unending. It is our blood, our bones, our kas.*

Thutmose sat carefully on the couch beside Meryet. Batiret had stilled her weeping, but she kept her face turned away from Pharaoh and Great Royal Wife alike.

"It is a terrible thing I do, Meryet. And yet, can I do any differently?"

Pain made Meryet's face gaunt and sickly. "I can see no other way."

He hung his head in defeat. "Hatshepsut, forgive me. She must forgive me. She must understand."

Meryet laid a hand on his shoulder. Thutmose felt how it trembled, felt the weight of regret sink from her flesh into his own. Guilt and duty. They were braided together as tightly as the fibers of a rope. Thutmose knew the work that awaited him, knew the obligation he must tend to, though it stabbed deep into his heart with a pain that no eternity could ever abate. He thought of his son, growing into the inheritance Thutmose had worked so hard to secure. He thought of Hatshepsut keening her regrets, cursing even the divinity that was inside herself. He thought of Egypt, kept whole and safe by the terrible sacrifices Hatshepsut had made.

When he rose up to see to his task, he did so abruptly, strong, decided, a cobra rearing from the sand.

Epilogue

IN THE BLUE CHILL BEFORE dawn, a heavy mist hung above the slick dark mirror of the Iteru. It would dissipate quickly as Re rode his golden barque into the morning sky, but by then Thutmose would be gone, sailing north at the head of his mighty war fleet. He stared down the water steps, parting the veils of fog with his eyes, searching for the solid shape of his fastest ship. The mist was too thick to permit a view of the boat, but he knew it was moored there, waiting for him as it had so many times before, on so many mornings like this one, dense with river haze and expectation.

"And so you are going away again." Meryet gave a dramatic sigh, but she smiled at him. The years had not diminished her beauty, though time on the throne had hardened her features. It was a pleasant enough hardness, the sharp definition and unbreakable countenance of a goddess carved in stone.

No – not stone. Stone breaks all too easily. Thutmose knew by now how easily stone cracked, how it smoothed beneath the cruel bite of the chisel. Meryet would never break.

Beside his wife, Amunhotep bounced on the balls of his feet. He was seven years old now, growing fast, taller than Thutmose could believe. "When do I get to sail with you, Father? I want to go to war!"

Thutmose raised the boy's chin in his hand, savored the precious sight of him in his childhood sidelock, the sweet roundness of his face. "Don't be in such a hurry to grow up,

Amunhotep." *Amun knows you're doing it fast enough already.*

The prince scowled. "Well, I am in a hurry. Waset is boring. I want to fight in the north like you!"

"I know."

"Your time will come," Meryet assured him. She took Thutmose's hand. "I will keep your throne warm until you return."

He laughed and swept her into his arms, kissed her long and deep until Amunhotep groaned in protest.

"I'll hurry back," Thutmose promised.

"As soon as you've made Egypt a little bigger; I know. Be safe, Thutmose. Go with the gods."

The mist parted for him as he made his way down the water steps. His great war boat rocked eagerly in its moorings, its cedar nose reaching high and arrogant above the fierce Eye of Horus that stared at him from the prow. After so many campaigns both up and down the river, the ship was his oldest friend, save for Meryet. His feet found the ramp as easily as his hands could find the hilt of his sword or the haft of his spear.

The pre-dawn lights of Waset receded into a black, mist-shrouded distance as his rowers struck out for the middle of the Iteru, where the northward current ran fast and deep. Thutmose took up his favorite position in the ship's prow. He watched the sun rise, a gathering glow piercing through the fog, a golden light spreading across the horizon, illuminating the mist with such ferocity that he had to drop his eyes from the sky to the ship's rail.

He studied his own hands where they lay on the gilded rail, lifted one to inspect beneath his nails. He had scrubbed and scrubbed his hands in his bath that morning, as he did every morning and every night. There was not a speck of stone dust beneath Thutmose's nails, and yet he could feel the accusing grit of altered and destroyed monuments there, and everywhere on his body, pressing into his flesh, stinging against his skin. He could feel the grains of dust that had once been Hatshepsut's image, Hatshepsut's name – her kas. The sense of her destruction never left his body, a palpable discomfort, a weight around his neck.

But Amunhotep's inheritance was secure. The legacy of Thutmose the First would go on into eternity. It was Hatshepsut's legacy, too – she was a part of all he did, all he achieved – she who had been a mother to Thutmose.

He lifted a small leather pouch that hung from his sword belt. The drawstrings were stiff with the dirt of many foreign roads, many campaigns past, but his fingers knew how to work them open. Inside was his small treasure, the seed he would plant when he reached the lands far beyond Retjenu, beyond Ugarit, stretching away to the north and east, the new borders he had laid to expand Egypt out across the whole of the earth. He lifted the treasure out of the bag, examined it on his palm.

It was a stone scarab – not large, carved in simple granite, not bright turquoise or lapis or brilliant deep malachite, river-green. It was plain, but strong; enduring enough to last centuries unchanged, so long as no chisel or hammer found it. He studied the shape of the scarab's wings, the intricate detail of its feathered antennae folded back across its rounded body. Thutmose turned it over in his hand.

On the flat reverse side was a name, encircled by the cartouche of royalty. He traced the familiar characters with his thumb. *Maatkare Hatshepsut.*

How many of these scarabs had he left in his wake, planted like hopeful vines across the expanding frontier? How many small tablets that bore her name and titles, how many tiny statues of her image, striding as bold as a god? Dozens. He would hide this one in the earth somewhere, in a cave, if he found one, or bury it on a hilltop just beneath the surface where the sun's rays could reach through the dust and warm her name, bring her back to life. Her name intact, fixed into eternal stone.

He hoped it was enough to atone for what he did in the temples and courts of the Two Lands, scraping her from history with the stroke of his workmen's chisels.

Thutmose slipped the scarab back into his pouch, tightened the strings carefully so it would not be lost. Too much of her was lost already. Many nights he had lain awake, imagining her kas scattered, torn loose from their familiar stone moorings in the Black Land. He pictured her forlorn kas wandering, disjointed and confused but not dead. Never dead, so long as he had his scarabs to plant in the earth, his little statues.

It was a very small comfort to him.

A far greater comfort was the battle to come. War was his only balm now, the only cure for the deep, aching wound in his ka, a wound as deep as if it had been carved by one of his own chisels. Yes, he was strong, and he gloried in his strength and his strategy. He would add more lands to Egypt's territory; of this he had no doubt.

But he did not fight merely for the sake of it, nor push the borders of the Two Lands ever outward to increase his wealth or his infamy among the world's lesser kings.

He did it for the sake of his scarabs – for the sake of her name.

For he had destroyed every one of her monuments that he could reach, erased her name from obelisks and temple walls. He did it for the sake of Egypt, ah – but knowing his reason was just did not ease the burden of his guilt.

If he must banish her kas from the Two Lands, if he must erase her memory from the hearts of men, then he would expand his empire until it was so great that Hatshepsut's lost kas would never find themselves without Egyptian gods. He would make all the world his, and no matter where Hatshepsut wandered, she would never be without the light of Amun-Re to guide her home.

My command stands firm like the mountains; the sun's disc shines upon my royal name. My falcon rises high above the kingly banner, eternally.

> *-Inscription from the Temple of Pakhet by Hatshepsut, fifth king of the Eighteenth Dynasty*

HISTORICAL NOTES

Please, gentle readers! Set down your pitchforks and torches! I swear I meant no harm; I only wanted to entertain you.

All right, I admit I got somewhat creative with history this time around, even more creative than I dared to be with the previous books in this series. In fact, I will confess that I've felt a persistent pang of worry over that whole Satiah/Neferure thing ever since I first came up with the idea back in 2008, when I started putting together The She-King inside my head. I knew I'd be taking a gamble with readers' patience; all I could do was hope I could make the story engaging enough that my readers would be willing to venture with me into the realm of truly wild speculation.

In my defense, it's not an *entirely* absurd plot device. Thutmose III was probably married to Neferure at one point. After Neferure vanished from history, she was replaced with a Great Royal Wife by the name of Satiah. On one monument, Satiah appears with startling prominence – much greater prominence than any queen was ever given in ancient Egypt, before or since – although it's not entirely clear whether the original version of the monument always depicted Satiah, or whether it was first meant to represent Neferure, and Satiah co-opted the monument later. Either way, my trick of making Neferure and Satiah interchangeable is supported by history, albeit in a very roundabout and tenuous way.

Thutmose III did have a son named Amenemhat, and

some Egyptologists believe that Satiah was his mother, while others speculate that Amenemhat came from the union of Thutmose III and Neferure. You can see where my inspiration for the Satiah/Neferure tangle came from.

My other affronts to history, in this book at least, are minor by comparison.

I moved the Battle of Megiddo (still a famous enough example of strategy, I hear, that it's taught in modern military schools) forward in time by about two years. It was actually staged about two years after Hatshepsut's death, but because it was such a dramatic and bloody battle, I wanted to use it as an expression of Thutmose's grief and rage over Hatshepsut's demise and his own perceived part in her downfall. For my purposes, the battle had to come immediately after the lady Pharaoh went to the big barque in the sky.

And finally, Hatshepsut's reign actually lasted twenty-two years (I have her ruling for about twenty-one.) It's a remarkably complicated trick, to make real history align with the pacing of an entertaining story. For the purposes of fiction, I figured twenty-one years was pretty darn close to good enough.

I promise more fidelity to actual history in my next novel. Honest.

Notes on the Language Used

This novel is set in historical Egypt, about 1500 years before the Common Era and roughly 1200 years before Alexander the Great conquered the Nile. With the dawning of the Greek period, a shift in the old Egyptian language began. Proper nouns (and, we can assume, other parts of the language) took on a decidedly Greek bent, which today most historians use when referring to ancient Egyptians and their world.

This presents a bit of a tangle for a historical novelist like myself. Culturally, we are familiar with Greek-influenced names like Thebes, Rameses, and Isis. In fact, even the name Egypt is not Egyptian; it has a long chain of derivations through Greek, Latin, and French. However, the historic people in my novel would have scratched their heads over such foreign words for their various places, people, and gods. And linguistically, the modern English-speaking reader will probably have a difficult time wrapping her head and tongue around such tricky names as Djhtms – an authentic and very common man's name for the time and place where Sovereign of Stars is set (rather the equivalent of a Mike or Tom or Jim).

On the balance, cultural authenticity is important to me, and so I've reverted to ancient Egyptian versions of various proper nouns and other words in the majority of cases. A glossary of ancient Egyptian words used in this book, and their more familiar Greco-English translations, follows.

In some cases, to avoid headaches and to preserve (I hope) the flow of the narrative, I have kept modernized versions of certain words in spite of their inauthentic nature. Notably, I use Egypt rather than the authentic Kmet. It is a word that instantly evokes the reader's own romantic perceptions of the land and time, whatever those may be, and its presence in the story can only aid my own attempts at world-building. I have opted for the fairly Greeky, English-friendly name Thutmose in place of Djhtms, which is simply a tongue-twister; and the word Pharaoh, which is French in origin (the French have always been enthusiastic Egyptologists) rather than the Egyptian pra'a, simply because Pharaoh is such a familiar word in the mind of a contemporary reader. Wherever possible, I have used "Pharaoh" sparingly, only to avoid repetitiveness, and have instead opted for the simple translation of "king." I've also decided, after much flip-flopping, to use the familiar Greek name Horus for the falcon-headed god, rather than the authentic name Horu. The two are close, but in every case reading Horu in my sentences interrupted the flow and tripped me up. Horus flies more smoothly on his falcon wings; ditto for Hathor, who should properly be called Hawet-Hor, but seems to prefer her modernized name.

As always, I hope the reader appreciates these concessions to historical accuracy and to comfort.

Glossary

ankh – the breath of life; the animating spirit that makes humans live

Anupu – Anubis

deby – hippopotamus

Djeser-Djeseru – "Holiest of Holies," the name of Hatshepsut's mortuary temple, known today as Dier-el Bahri.

Heqa-Khasewet – Hyksos

Ipet-Isut – "Holy House"; the temple complex at Karnak

Iset – Isis

Iteru – Nile

Iunet – Dendera

ka – not quite in line with the Western concept of a "soul" or "spirit," a ka was an individual's vital essence, that which made him or her live.

Kush – Nubia

maat – A concept difficult for modern Westerners to accurately define: something like righteousness, something like divine order, something like justice. It is to a sense of "God is in His Heaven and all is right with the world" as the native Hawai'ian word *aloha* is to an overall feeling of affection, pleasure, well-being, and joyful anticipation. It is also the name of the goddess of the concept – the goddess of "what is right."

mawat – mother; also used to refer to mother-figures such as nurses

Medjay – An Egyptian citizen of Nubian descent

rekhet – people of the common class; peasants

sepat – nome, or district

seshep – sphinx

sesheshet – sistrum; ceremonial rattle

tjati – vizier; governor of a sepat or district

Waser – Osiris, god of the afterlife, the underworld, and the dead. Also used as a prefix when referring to a deceased king.

Waset – Thebes

Acknowledgments

I spent most of my adult life striving to make a career writing books. During all those years, I worked at the oddest variety of jobs – any job, just to keep a roof over my head and food in my fridge – while I honed my craft and wrote my books. Some of my jobs were tolerable. Some were exotic and kind of fun. Most were a misery and I couldn't wait to leave.

What a cruel irony, then, that in the year when my books finally took off and I was at last able to make my lifelong dream a reality, I ended up at a job I truly loved.

Every single person at Trupanion has been a delight to work with – something that can't be said of most workplaces, especially not with companies as large and growing as this one. And yet it's true: each individual is amazing. Many are good friends to me now. Some are as close as family.

I wouldn't be the person I am today without the friendship of my co-workers at Trupanion: Emily Renfrew, Erin Milholland, Forrest Downey, Whitney Drake, Cuppy Taylor, Connie Park, Emily Burns, Jessica Rogers, Diana Moreno, Crystal Alvarez, Stephanie Manzo, Julie Coulter, Heather Pike, Chrissy Barger, Diana Cross, Paulette Molnar, Pamela Olsen, Jenn Lach, Jayme Markham, Kelly Maheu, Bridget Lombardo, and Tuesday Reimers. Plus Shannon, whose last name I haven't learned yet (sorry, Shannon.) And, of course, Nemo, Paisley, Dizzy, Romeo, Cole, Tank, Athena, Cyrus, Mr. Tibbs, Gizmo, Bishop, Iris, Butters, Half Pint, Cherry Bomb,

Gary the Longdog, Steeeven, and The Dread Pirate Roberts.

I love you all *so much*, and I'm really going to miss you, every single day.

Thanks as always to Paul Harnden, who puts up with so much and still manages to get excited about everything I write. Off we go on the first adventure of many.

-Libbie

About the Author

Libbie Hawker is the author of seven books, with many more on the way. Her historical novels have enjoyed more than three years of steady presence on Top 100 lists in the largest bookstore in the world, and Hawker has become a leading voice in independent historical fiction, where she strives to recreate the drama and humanity of the past with literary style and authentic atmosphere.

She is terrified of elephants, loves the American west, and hates sushi. Although she currently lives in Seattle, by the time you read this she may be residing on San Juan Island.

Find more information about her books at LibbieHawker. com

Made in the USA
Columbia, SC
17 March 2018